The Posse

TAWDRA KANDLE

The Posse
Copyright © 2013 Tawdra Kandle

All rights reserved.

Cover/Interior Design by Champagne Book Design

ISBN: 978-1-68230-263-7

Dedication

To Cheryl, Sally, Ellen and Terry
The bravest women I know.

The Posse

Prologue

NOTE: The Posse was originally written in the third person.
It has been re-edited to the first person in order to match
with the other books in the series.
If you would prefer to read it in its original third person
POV, you can go *here* and download a free copy.

Logan

"To Daniel."

"To Daniel." Five glasses clinked together, but instead of the raucous laughter and jives that would normally have followed such a toast, there was only silence. The men around the bar looked at the floor, the wall or into their glasses—any place but at each other, where someone might have to acknowledge the deep sadness sunk into each face.

Eric Fleming sniffed once, long and loud. "Can't believe it's been a year."

"Hell of a year for Jude, too," put in Matt Spencer.

"The real hell for her was the year before." I reached beneath the bar and pulled out another bottle of beer. "Taking care of Daniel, watching him disappear right in front of her."

We all nodded, wagging our heads in unison. No one in this crowd would ever dispute the way Jude Hawthorne had nursed her husband during his fight with cancer.

"Dammit, did you see her face today? When we let go his ashes? I'm telling you, I've never seen anything sadder. But she held it together, man. Like she always did. Like she always does." Cooper Davis rubbed a hand over his eyes.

"Hell of a woman," Matt said.

"To Jude." Mark Rivers held out his beer. "My baby sister. She and Daniel. . ." His voice trailed, and he coughed. "They were amazing together."

"What's she going to do now?" Cooper dropped his empty into a nearby barrel and popped another top. "I mean, she's holding onto the Tide, right? She's not going to sell?"

Mark shook his head. "Nah, why should she? It's hers. It belongs to our family."

"I think the Tide and the kids are what kept her going this last year." I traced the path of a drop of condensation down the side of my glass. "She won't give that up."

"The kids are going back to school, right?" said Eric.

"Yeah, Meggie's heading up to Savannah this weekend, and Joseph is driving to Gainesville with some friends next week." Mark stood and stretched. "I gotta head home. Back to school tomorrow."

"You can't go now. I've still got a bottle of Jack and three six-packs." I glanced around the room. "Plus, we're not ready yet. To end this."

Mark sat down again without argument. Going home would mean more than the end of just the evening. Even though we had left the last of Daniel's ashes in the rolling waves of the Atlantic that afternoon, as long as we remained here in Logan's house, talking about our friend, he wasn't really gone. Once we left, it would be over.

The posse would be finished.

"What if Jude doesn't stay?" Eric spoke up from his perch in the corner. "What if she meets someone?"

"Who's she going to meet here in Crystal Cove?" Mark shrugged. "And I don't think she's even interested in that kind of thing."

"Not now. But she's not exactly a washed-up old lady, you know? And people come to the Cove. Tourists. Someone could stop at the Tide for breakfast, sweep her off her feet—"

Cooper laughed. "You been hitting the romance stack at the library again, Eric? Sweep her off her feet, huh?"

Matt took a long pull of his beer. "Could happen. Stranger things, you know."

Mark shook his head. "Jude won't leave. Her life is here."

"Daniel was her life," I said. "And he's gone."

"She can't. If Jude leaves, the posse is done for real." Eric's mouth twisted into a worried frown.

We were silent again, each considering. If any of us was tempted to point out that with Daniel's death, over thirty years of unbroken friendship was gone anyway, no one did. Jude had always been an unofficial member. She stood for Daniel now; there wasn't any need to voice that.

"What can we do?" Mark slumped back into his chair, covering his eyes. "Free world. We can't *make* her stay. If she meets someone else, falls in love—or whatever, what are we going to do? Tell her no? As her big brother, I can promise you that doesn't fly."

"It could be us. One of us could be the one to sweep her off her feet." Matt's words were measured, careful. "I mean, why not? We've all known each other forever. If I was married and then I was—well, wasn't here anymore, I'd want one of you guys to take care of my wife."

"Daniel asked us to look after her." Cooper poured another glass of whiskey. "I guess that's true."

"Seriously?" I shook my head. "What is this, the Middle Ages? Our friend dies, so one of has to jump into his spot. Since when do we buy into arranged marriages?"

"Who said anything about marriage?" Matt asked. "But a relationship between two consenting adults—old friends, who know everything about each other—why not? Why wouldn't it work?"

They all mulled it over. It was crazy, but we'd done worse. And when we thought about Daniel, about Jude. . .there wasn't anything any one of us wouldn't do.

"So who goes for it?" Cooper was the first one to speak. "How do we figure that out? Draw straws? Pissing contest?"

"Well, Eric and I are both out. Wives might raise a fuss, plus—" Mark hooked two thumbs to his chest. "Brother. It's between the rest of you."

"Why don't we let Jude choose?" I flickered my eyes between Cooper and Matt.

"Are you crazy? Jude will never agree to that." Matt rolled his eyes.

"I don't mean we tell her. I mean, we all. . .you know. . .like, date her. What do all the girls say? Court her. And whoever clicks, that's the one." I flipped up a hand.

"You, me and Cooper?" Matt nodded. "Okay. Hey, I got nothing to lose. It's not like women are beating down the door."

"If Jude gets wind of this, she'll blow a gasket." Mark crumbled his napkin, aimed for the trash can and missed.

"I think we can keep it quiet. Nice shot, by the way." Cooper punched his friend in the shoulder.

"Basketball's not my game. But listen, I'm serious. How are you going to keep this from her? Take turns?"

"No." I spoke definitively. "We act natural. We do what we would anyway—check in with her, take her to dinner, whatever. And then we see what happens."

"And no hard feelings, right? No matter who she chooses. We say it right up front now, Jude is the final word. Agreed?" Cooper laid a hand on the oak bar, a gesture that was old as our friendship. Matt slapped his own hand down on top, followed by Eric and Mark. I was last, unfurling a fist on the pile.

"Deal," I said. "Now let's break out the good stuff."

Chapter One

Jude

THE BLACK VELVET SKY WAS giving way to vague bands of pink as I climbed up the cement steps that led to the side door of the Rip Tide. The restaurant sat at the edge of the beach, ugly and unassuming in its dingy white brick glory. When I was a little girl, I had thought the Tide looked as though it had grown out of the sidewalk and gravel parking lot. The raised porch that jutted over the sand had been added about ten years before I was born, so it was practically brand new. My dad screened it in just before my ninth birthday, and we'd had my party there that year.

As I did every morning, I took a moment, leaned against the bricks and looked out over the beach into the waves. I wondered how many times I'd done this, stood here at five AM and let the rare solitude wash over me.

I had been opening the Tide since the summer after I turned sixteen. For the first two years, I came in with my dad, riding shotgun in his old black pickup, learning how to start the day. When school resumed that fall, my father had given me the option to sleep that extra hour, but I had chosen to spend it with him instead. He never said it outright, but I knew he was proud of my choice.

After graduation, I took over opening on my own. My mother worried about me all alone on the dark mornings, but I overheard my father saying, "It's the Cove, Maggie. She'll be safe."

I didn't miss an opening until my wedding day, and only then because my mom put her foot down and insisted. Daniel and I spent our honeymoon in the mountains of Gatlinburg, a wedding gift given reluctantly by his parents, who hadn't been able to convince their son to wait until after college graduation to marry me.

I didn't miss opening the Tide the day I gave birth to Meghan, because my daughter had kindly waited to be born until eight in the evening. Joseph was another story; he'd made his appearance at four in the morning. I could still see Daniel, a full-day's growth of beard on his tired face, holding his son and grinning up at me.

"Hey, if you get up now, you could still make it to the Tide for opening," he'd teased, and exhausted from laboring for ten hours, I hadn't even had the strength to throw my pillow at him.

I took off four weeks after each of my children was born. And then I missed opening the day my mother died, because I wouldn't leave my dad and my brother Mark in that empty, hopeless hospital room where Maggie Rivers had just drawn her last breath.

I did open the Tide hours after my father passed, though, because I knew that was where he needed me and where I needed to be. I came the morning after Daniel had died, too. I couldn't stand being in that house one more minute, knowing I'd never see my husband again.

I smothered a sigh, gripping the chilled metal of the doorknob just as I heard my name.

"Jude!"

It was rare that anyone was out this early, and I turned in surprise, a frown between my eyes. It took a moment of focus to recognize the man jogging up the sand toward me.

"Good God, Logan, what the hell are you doing up so early? I thought you'd all be ringing in the wee small hours last night."

Logan had the good grace to look a little winded, even as he managed a grin. "We did. Around two, I gave up the ghost and told them to turn off the lights and lock up before they went to bed."

"Two? And you're up running at five?"

He shrugged. "The body clock won't be turned off. I couldn't get back to sleep, so I figured I'd get in a jog before everyone else woke up."

I unlocked the door. "I've got to get the grill on. Want some coffee? Or a bottle of water?"

"How about both?"

I shot him a grin as I flipped on lights and headed for the kitchen. Logan climbed onto a barstool, and I reached into the small fridge to pull out the water. I slid it across the bar to Logan and then moved through the kitchen, setting up the coffee and turning on the grills.

"You look like you could do all that with your eyes closed." Logan took a long chug on the water before recapping it.

I laughed. "Some mornings I do."

"Do you ever think about giving it up?"

"The mornings? Nah. Like you said, the body clock gets me up at four every morning anyway. I'd be awake worrying even if I turned it over to someone else."

Logan shook his head. "Not the mornings so much as the whole thing. Running the business."

"The Tide?" I snagged two mugs off a shelf and filled them with steaming coffee. "Give it up? No." I doctored Logan's coffee with a sugar and a healthy dose of cream before setting it in front of him.

Leaning my elbows on the bar, I blew into my own cup. "Funny, just before you showed up, I was thinking about how long I've been pulling morning duty. Almost thirty years, give or take. Some days I think. . .why? I want to stay in bed, I just want a day to myself. But you know, it's a part of me. Might be a pain in the neck sometimes, but it's who I am."

Logan watched me sip the coffee. My black hair was skinned back into a pony tail, just as it was every day, and even as I felt his eyes on me, my eyes stayed fastened on the dark wood of the bar top. With one finger, I traced an ancient gouge in the wood, but I was sure Logan knew I wasn't seeing it. I drew in a deep breath and set the mug on a coaster.

"So what time did my kids leave your house?"

He drank before answering. "Before midnight. You weren't up when they got home?"

"They crashed here, upstairs in the apartment. They were going to have a few friends come over, hang out. I wanted the peace."

Logan frowned. "I thought they were going to be with you last night. They left you alone?"

"Logan." I covered one of his large tanned hands with my own smaller one. "I'm telling you, I wanted some time. If I had said I needed them, you know they would've been there. They're good kids."

"Yeah, they are." He turned his hand beneath mine to grip it briefly. "You going to be okay when they go back to school?"

I returned the hand squeeze for just a minute before pulling loose and turning to the large refrigerator at the back of the kitchen.

"Yeah, I'll be fine. They need to go back. This last year, and the one before, it was tough on them. They need to go be kids again. We're all ready for it."

"Okay." Logan drained the last of his coffee and rounded the bar to rinse off the mug in the huge sink. "You know where we are if you need anything. All of us. You only have to ask."

"I do know." I shot him a smile. "Now get out of here and let me get cooking. The early birds are going to be here in a few minutes wanting their pancakes and eggs. And you have a house full of hung-over men you need to kick out."

"Right." Logan grabbed the bottle of water to take with him. "Thanks for the drinks, Jude."

As I watched him stride toward the door, the muscles on his back evident through the tight running shirt, light brown hair curling on his neck, I felt an almost foreign warmth shoot down my spine, straight to my knees. I paused for a moment to appreciate the view, and then shook my head.

Pull it together, Jude. Here comes the breakfast crowd.

Chapter Two

Jude

MEGHAN STUMBLED DOWN THE NARROW steps from the apartment over the Rip Tide. She yawned as she rounded the corner into the main dining room and plopped onto a bar stool.

I was across the room, chatting with a couple of tourists. I stood with one leg bent onto an empty chair so that I could point out something on the simple one-laminated-page menu.

"It all looks good," the woman told me. "It's just that my husband here wants lunch, and I was hoping to have breakfast."

"It's almost eleven. Too late for breakfast." The man shook his head.

I smiled. "I know it says we only serve breakfast until ten on weekdays, but I can whip you up some pancakes and eggs. How does that sound?"

"That would be perfect." The woman shot her husband a triumphant look, and he rolled his eyes.

"And how about one of our special Ripper burgers for you, sir?" I cocked my head.

"Sounds good." He handed me both of the menus, and I moved away from the table, back to the open kitchen.

"Hey, sleepy head," I greeted my daughter. "Late night?"

Meggie shrugged. "Not too bad. I'm just stocking up on sleep before I go back to school. I've got that early class every single day."

I placed my hand over my heart. "You poor child, having to get up before eight o'clock five days a week..."

"Whatever!" Meghan's grin softened the words. "Do you have any coffee back there?"

"What do you think?" I filled a mug for my daughter and slid it across the bar before getting to work on my customers' order. "Hey, Mack, would you make up a Ripper, please? I'll take care of the breakfast order."

The bald man standing in front of the griddle waved his spatula in acknowledgement and pulled a beef patty from the fridge. Meghan's nose wrinkled as the smell reached her.

At my end of the stove, I poured pancake batter into a pan and broke eggs into a bowl. My hand moved at lightning speed as I whipped them into a yellow froth.

Meghan frowned as she watched. "You know, you've always been in good shape, Mom, but the last two years, you've gone right past slender into skinny. Those shorts you always wear to work are downright baggy. And your arms are almost bony."

"Thanks." I shot her mock glare over my shoulder. "I appreciate the love."

Neither Joseph nor Meghan had inherited my dark hair,

but they both had my eyes and my bone structure. Meghan and I were both used to people commenting on how much she looked like me, but as I ventured a glance down at my own body, I realized that she was right. We used to weigh almost the same, but I wouldn't be surprised if she had a good ten pounds on me.

"Are you going to be okay, Mom?" Meggie blurted out the words, her eyes anxious. "When Joseph and I go back to school, I mean?"

I flipped a pancake and forced a wry grin. Catching my daughter's worried expression, I flung one hand over my forehead. "Oh, Meghan, after you've gone, whatever shall I do?"

Meggie scowled. "Shut up, I'm serious."

"Sweetie, you and your brother have gone away to college before. I've made it here without you. I love you, but I think I'll survive."

"Yeah, but before, you had Daddy." Even now, tears filled those green eyes, and I had to look away, busying myself with stacking pancakes and pouring the eggs into the hot pan.

"I'll be fine. I promise. Please don't worry."

"Will you be lonely, though? All I can think of is you, all by yourself, sitting in the big empty house."

"Nope. First of all, if I were, I would call up Aunt Janet and Aunt Sam, and we'd go hit the bars. Maybe that new male strip club in Daytona."

"Mom!" Meggie covered her ears. "That I don't want to hear."

I laughed. "And second, do you think the posse is going to leave me alone long enough to get lonely? Uncle Logan was here this morning when I opened. He claimed he couldn't help waking up, but I know him. He was making sure I was okay."

"That makes me feel better. It was just that Joseph and I were talking last night, and it hit me that we're really leaving you this time. Not just to come back at the weekend. I won't be back home until Thanksgiving."

"And that's the way it should be. I'm grateful that you came home about every weekend last year. And Joseph taking his classes this year at the community college was a blessing. But it's time you both got on with your life. It's what Daddy would want." I paused to plate the eggs, add an orange wedge garnish and turned to take the burger plate from Mack. "Speaking of your brother, was he awake when you came down?"

"Nah. I'll go toss his butt out of bed." Meggie rose as I carried plates to the waiting table. At the door to the stairway, she turned back around and dashed to me.

"I love you, Mama," she said, half-choking as she hugged me. She ran upstairs, passing Sadie as the older woman carried a tray of dishes into the sink area.

"You got a special girl there." Sadie wiped suspicious moisture from her eyes when I came back around the bar.

"Makes you wonder how that happened, doesn't it?" I teased.

"Sure does, 'cause you for sure were a mess when you were her age!" Sadie pulled the ball cap tighter over her grey hair.

I stopped for a minute, thinking. "I was married and pregnant with her when I was Meggie's age," I reminded the older woman.

"Yup. Like I said, a mess."

"Did I ever stop being a mess?"

Sadie pushed a glass against the iced tea dispenser, refilling it for her customer. She tilted her head, considering.

"Maybe you're not so bad as you were. You gonna clean that egg pan or leave it there to get hard?"

I shook my head and grabbed the pan. Some things never changed, I thought. I might own the Tide, I might be over forty, but Sadie still ruled the roost.

Chapter Three

Matt

I COULDN'T DECIDE WHAT TO DO.

I had walked back to the storage room at The Surf Line three times and returned to the main shop empty-handed three times. Karl, the high school junior who worked part-time at the store, glanced up when I stalked back the last time.

"Uh, Mr. Spencer, everything okay?"

"What? Oh. Yeah. I'm just trying to make up my mind about something." I ran one hand over my shaggy blond hair. "Karl, you got a girlfriend?"

The boy grinned. "Nah. My mom says I shouldn't get tied down. I just, you know, date. Meet girls, take them out. Why, do you have someone I should meet?"

I stared at him blankly for a minute. "No. Who would I want you to meet?"

Karl shrugged. "I don't know. You're friends with Meggie

Hawthorne. I thought maybe you might want to fix me up with her. She's hot."

"Meggie? My God, Karl, she's like my niece. I've known her since before she was born. I'm not looking to hook her up with you. And she's like four years older than you."

Karl smiled again, crinkling his blue eyes in his tan face. "I like older women."

I rolled my eyes. "I just bet. Well, Meghan went back to Savannah today, so you're out of luck." I moved over to fix one of the displays and then leaned out the door, looking down the sidewalk.

"You looking for someone?"

"I'm trying to decide—" I sighed and bit the bullet. "Karl, what do you say to a girl when you want to ask her out? On a date?"

Understanding washed over Karl's face. "Mr. S., you *like* someone?"

I waved his hand. "None of your business."

"Well, you just asked me, so—"

"Karl, you know how I let you do consulting with some of the customers? Give them advice on surfing? Think of it like that. I need to consult with you, but you don't need details."

"Okay." The boy nodded. "So when I want to ask a girl to go out with me, I say something nice first. You know, like she's pretty, or she looks hot, or I like her hair. Girls like that. It softens them up. And then if I know there's something we both like to do, I ask her if she wants to go with me to do it. Like, you know, we both play Xbox or we like the same music. And then. . ." He spread it hands. "It just kind of happens from there."

"It happens? What happens? No." I put up both hands. "Never mind. I don't want to know. I was seventeen once. About a thousand years ago, I think."

I glanced outside again and took a deep breath. "Karl, keep your eye on things here. I've got to go down the street for a little bit. I'll be right back."

I strode out, well aware that Karl was probably going to scramble over to the door to see where I was heading the minute my back was turned. I could just imagine how rumors would begin, what people would say.

Matt Spencer's sniffing around after Jude Hawthorne. How long's it been since his friend Daniel died?

With a growl deep in my chest, I jerked open the door to the old restaurant and stalked inside.

I had been walking into the Tide for more years than I cared to remember. My dad brought me to the restaurant for breakfast every Saturday when I was a little boy, calling it our man time, a once-a-week escape from a house full of females. Then when I was old enough to ride my bike to the beach, I had joined Daniel, Cooper, Eric and Logan on summer days, dropping our bicycles near Mark's in the side of the parking lot. Mr. Rivers let us sit up at the bar while he served us chips and soda. He used to grouse about Mark getting distracted from his busboy job when his friends descended on the place, but then he always let his son leave with us and run down to the beach.

I'd brought my first date to the Tide, too, I remembered. Lonnie Severnson was the leggy blonde I'd finally asked out at the end of freshman year. I had been so nervous when I took her in, hoping against hope that none of my friends would be there that Friday night. As it was, only Jude and Daniel were in the restaurant. Jude was working tables, and Daniel sat at the corner of the bar, books open. Even then, before they'd officially become a couple, neither of them had eyes for anyone else.

But Jude had been kind that evening, talking to Lonnie and taking our order without any of the winks or leers I had dreaded. And Daniel only offered a grin and wave before his eyes fastened back on Jude as she wove between the tables with all the grace of a ballerina.

Remembering that gave me the courage I needed to make my way into the Rip Tide. It was the afternoon lull. In the height of the season, the place would be full, but now, with everything winding down, kids going back to school, there was only an older couple, sitting by a window with burgers and fries, and a few locals at the bar.

Jude was bent over the grill, scraping it with a long-handled blade. She stopped to blow a tendril of hair off her forehead and wiped the side of her face with the back of her hand. Spotting me, she smiled.

"Hey, Matty! What's going on?"

The nickname was a leftover from elementary school, and I tolerated it from a select few. I eased up on a barstool and tried to remember the words I'd planned on the way over.

"Not much. Quiet here."

She grinned. "Just a little. How's it down your end of the street?"

I lifted one shoulder. "About the same. We got a surfer meet this weekend, though, so it's going to be busy."

Jude dried her hands on a towel, reached under the bar and pulled out a bottle. She popped the cap and slid it across to me.

Yes. Liquid courage. I took a long swig and then tilted the neck toward Jude. "Join me?"

"I've got another two hours before Emmy takes over for the night, so I'm sticking to water." Jude lifted the bottle and drank.

I watched her closely. I tried to figure out whether or not the slim column of her neck above the black scoop neck shirt struck a chord. Did I feel anything for Jude other than the warm affection we'd always shared?

There was only one way to find out. I chugged down more of my beer and took a deep breath. "So the kids went back this morning? Both of them?"

"Yes." Jude sighed. "Joseph was supposed to wait until Monday, but he's living in an apartment with a bunch of guys, and one of them decided to bring down a truckload of furniture today. He needed help moving it in, and I think Joseph was ready to go. So. . .yeah. The nest is empty once again."

I nodded. "Do you want to have dinner with me tonight?"

Jude's eyebrows rose. "Dinner?"

"Yeah." I worked hard to keep my tone nonchalant. "You know, it's that meal at the end of the day. We can go over to that new Italian place in Elson. I've been wanting to try it."

She leaned against the bar, frowning. "Matt, you take out a different girl every week. Why haven't you taken one of them there?"

"You don't take a date to an Italian place on the first date, Jude. Too much garlic. You got to wait until a month or two in."

Jude laughed. "Okay. And you never get that far in."

I had the grace to feel a little uncomfortable. "Not recently, no."

"But I'm safe. I get it. All right, you got a deal. Can you give me until seven? Emmy gets here at five, and I'd like a little while to unwind, shower off the day."

"Sure." I felt extraordinarily lighter. "I'll pick you up at your house. See you then. Thanks for this." I drained the rest of the bottle and pushed it across the bar.

Outside in the sunshine, I walked back toward the store with more spring in my step. I paused just beyond the door to the Tide and squinted down the block at the bright yellow house that was fronted by scaffolding. It was going to be a bed and breakfast, the last project Holt/Hawthorne had undertaken before Daniel died.

I caught sight of a familiar figure in a suit moving to the front of the house. Logan was making one of his frequent visits, checking on progress. He stood looking up at the second floor, and as he turned to point something out to a passing workman, he saw me.

Logan stood completely still for a moment, and I imagined I could see his eyes flick to the door of the Rip Tide and then back to me. He raised one hand in a quick wave and then looked back at the yellow house.

The relief I had felt moments before dimmed just a bit before I went back to the surf shop.

Chapter Four

Jude

HIRING EMMY CARTER TO COVER Friday and Saturday nights at the Tide had been one of my more ingenious decisions. I realized that every week when Emmy strode through the door and took charge.

Emmy was in her mid-thirties. She was a local girl who had married a pro surfer when she was barely out of her teens. Ten years and three kids later, he left her to move to Hawaii, where the waves were bigger and life was easier. Emmy could've moved back with her parents, but instead she started her own business, baking pies out of her kitchen.

I was always eager to support local businesses, so it was a no-brainer to buy a few of the pies for my lunch crowd. One day Emmy delivered three peach pies on a late Friday afternoon, when the dinner rush was just getting underway. She stood for a moment in the door, watching me hustle as I shouted orders over the talk and music.

The next day, Emmy showed up during the afternoon lull, marched straight to the bar and leveled a determined gaze at me.

"You open this place up at six AM. And how many nights do you close before midnight?"

I raised an eyebrow. "We close at five in the afternoon except on Fridays and Saturdays."

"Okay." Emmy nodded. "So those two nights you close when?"

I shrugged. "Usually after one in season. Not as late during off."

"I have a proposal. Hire me to cover your night hours."

"I must have forgotten putting the help wanted sign on the window," I said. "I've never had anyone managing here on a permanent basis except me. Why should I change now?"

Emmy set her chin. "Because you deserve a break now and then. Because your kids are getting to the age where they need you around on weekends." She took a deep breath. "Because I need a little extra income while I'm getting this business up and running."

I held her eyes. "All good points. I'll think about it."

And I did. But giving up any control of the Tide was a hard thing. It was Daniel who gave me the final push.

"It would be nice to go away for a weekend or even just overnight once in a while. Plus, you know you want to help out Emmy. Give it a try. If it doesn't work, no harm done."

Far from it. Emmy had taken the job and run with it. She'd added dinner specials, brought in local bands to play, and streamlined our processes. From five to eight, The Tide was still a family friendly spot with kids-eat-free meals. But after eight, the lights dimmed, the music went up and The Rip Tide became one of the hottest restaurants on the beach.

Emmy's innovations brought in enough revenue to more than cover her salary, and I never looked back.

Now I watched my night-time manager weave her way to the bar, a bright smile on her face. Emmy's red hair was up in a messy bun, and she wore her usual green T-shirt and jeans.

"Get going, boss-lady." She bumped her shoulder against mine. "You've got a quiet house and hours of downtime. Go watch some old eps of *Burn Notice* or *Buffy*. You know I live vicariously through you."

"Ha." I pulled my handbag out from under the counter. "Sure, you do. Actually, I'm going out to dinner with Matt tonight, so no quiet for me."

"Matt?" Emmy's brows shot up. "Really?" She dragged out the word.

"Yes, really." I shook my head. "Emmy, I've known Matt Spencer for more years than you've been alive, probably. He and the rest of the posse are just keeping their eyes on me. He knew Meggie and Joseph went back to school today, so he's trying to keep me from being lonely."

"Hmm." Emmy's skepticism wasn't hard to detect. "Whatever you say, Miss Jude." She swatted at me. "Now get out of here. You're cramping my style. And you've got a date to get ready for."

"I'm telling you, it's not a date!" I rolled her eyes as I rounded the bar. "I'll have my phone if you need anything. Be careful, have a good night. Make lots of money."

It was my typical Friday night send-off, and Emmy waved me out the door.

The house that Daniel had built me was only about five minutes from The Tide. We had lived in the apartment above the restaurant until a few months before Joseph was born, but Daniel was determined that our house would be one of the first projects undertaken by the new company he'd formed with Logan. Our friend had loved designing the house almost as much as Daniel had enjoyed making the plans a reality. It was simple and eminently livable, laid out on one story with lots of windows. We'd added the pool and landscaping when the kids were in elementary school, and for our twentieth wedding anniversary, Daniel had installed a sound system that ran throughout the entire house and backyard.

"So you can indulge your love for what passed for music in the eighties," he'd teased. I had pretended to be insulted, even as I began making play lists in my head.

Walking in now from the garage, I dropped my bag on a chair and headed for the kitchen. I pulled a bottle of water out of the fridge and wandered out onto the lanai.

It was quiet, and I thought it would have been a perfect night to enjoy takeout from my own restaurant here by the pool, along with a lovely glass of Riesling. I could finish the book I'd been falling asleep over for the past week. Call the kids and make sure they'd made it to Gainesville and Savannah.

But no, instead I was going to haul my cookies back to my bedroom, scrounge up something decent to wear and go to a restaurant, the last place I wanted to be on my night off. I was going to put on a big smile and convince Matt that I was doing okay so that he could take that info back to the rest of the posse, and maybe I'd get a little peace.

I sighed and drained the water from my bottle. Stalling just a little, I pulled my phone out and checked messages. Sure enough, there were several: two from Meggie, reporting the progress of her drive, and one line from Joseph that simply said, "*We r here.*"

I smiled, missing them already, and texted back quickly. "Good to know. Having dinner with U Matt. Be safe, love you. Talk soon."

And then because I couldn't put it off anymore, I pushed to my feet and went back to find something to wear, pausing only long enough to turn on my music so that it blasted from the kitchen to the bedroom.

Florida beach dinner attire was simple. There were few places where I couldn't wear shorts, but since it was Friday night and Matt was going to the trouble of taking me to dinner, I found a sundress that was both pretty and comfortable. I paired it with flat beaded sandals and some gold hoop earrings and decided I'd done my best.

Dressing after a quick shower, I braided my hair, spritzed on perfume and grabbed a sweater. It was a given that the a/c at the restaurant would be running overtime; I never went out to eat without a jacket of some kind.

David Bowie began singing about modern love over the speakers. I smiled, thinking that this was one huge benefit of having the house to myself. There were no kids to roll their eyes or moan, "Mom, seriously?"

Dancing by the full-length mirror that hung on my

bathroom door, I came to a halt. The last time I'd been dressed up for anything was Daniel's funeral, over a year ago. I frowned at my own image, at the bones jutting out of my shoulders, the hollows in my neck. Eating had not been a priority for the last few years, but I hadn't realized that the weight loss was so pronounced until Meghan had pointed it out last week.

The doorbell rang, jolting me away from the self-study. Matt stood on the brick porch, hands in the pockets of his khakis. He wore a black shirt, open at the neck, with the sleeves rolled to his elbows.

His smile didn't quite reach his eyes as I opened the door, calling out to him.

"Hey! Hold on, let me grab my bag and my keys and turn off the music. I'll be right there."

Matt stood aside as I locked the door and turned toward the driveway. He almost ran into my back when I stopped suddenly.

"Oh my God, you brought the 'Vette!" I turned around, hand to my mouth.

Matt grinned. "I wasn't going to make you climb into the Jeep. Besides, you all give me so much shit about it, I figured it was about time you took a ride."

I followed him to the car and climbed in when he held the door. I ran one hand over the dash, smiling. Matt had bought the car after his divorce, and all the posse had teased him mercilessly about being a stereotypical middle-aged divorced man. He'd taken it in stride, I'd thought, but seeing it now, I realized he'd never had any of us take a ride in it, never drove it around us after he first bought it.

Matt dropped into the driver's seat and turned the key. He backed out of the driveway, one hand on the headrest of my seat, and I caught a whiff of his scent, a mix of cologne and lingering sunscreen. It was both disconcertingly familiar and jarringly foreign; I knew it as Matt's particular smell, and yet I was unused to it in such close quarters. For the first time, I felt unsettled about this evening, as Emmy's teasing words rang in my ears.

"In the mood for some garlic?" Matt slid a sideways grin my way, and I felt a little better. This was Matty, after all. I still saw him as the earnest little boy who came for breakfast every Saturday with his dad.

"Sounds good," I said, shifting in my seat. "I just hope I don't bore you to death or fall asleep. Daniel used to say I was pretty useless on Friday nights. The whole week just seems to catch up with me."

I hadn't meant to bring up Daniel as a defense against any ideas Matt might have, but not talking about him would have been unnatural. Matt didn't seem to mind. He lifted one shoulder.

"That's okay. If you conk out on me, I'll carry you home."

We were quiet for a moment then, both lost in our own thoughts. I searched for something else to say, annoyed that I felt I had to make small talk.

"The kids got to school without any problem," I heard myself say. "I bet they're happy to be back with their friends."

Matt took a smooth corner. "Meggie's finishing this year, right? And what happens with Joseph now? Does he lose any time with taking his classes here last year?"

I nodded, pursing my lips. "Just a little. He'll be about a

semester behind, unless he takes summer classes next year to catch up. I didn't want him to take the leave, but when he insisted. . .well, it was good to have him living home with me this last year. Even with Meggie coming home every weekend, the between times would have been harder without Joseph. But I hope he doesn't regret it."

"He won't. He's a good kid." Matt turned the car into a small parking lot next to a two-story house that was flooded with lights. People stood in the side garden, holding drinks, and a line snaked around the porch.

"Wow, this place is hopping," I said as we made our way up the steps. "Wonder how long we'll have to wait." My stomach growled on cue, and Matt laughed.

"No wait for us. I called ahead. I have a friend here." He led me to the podium and gave his name to the maitre' d, who grinned and pointed us inside.

Just within the doors, a hostess waited with two menus in hand. "Good evening, Mr. Spencer! Won't you come this way?"

We followed her down a narrow hall to a wide room in the back. The light was dim, and several other couples sat at tables for two. Matt held my chair, and once again I had that sense of foreboding.

This is not a date. This is one of my oldest friends taking me out to dinner so I don't have to be alone the day my kids left.

I scanned the menu, trying to focus my mind on food and not the tumbling feeling in my stomach. My eyes caught on one entry in the appetizers column as I remembered what Matt had told me earlier.

"Why don't we get some of this roasted garlic to start? It

looks good." *Ordering garlic should make it clear that I know this isn't a real date.*

Matt glanced at me, a furrow between his brows. He nodded and turned to the waitress who appeared tableside.

"We'll start with the roasted garlic, and Jude, what do you want to drink?"

"Ahhh. . ." I looked at the wine list. "Just a glass of the house white, please."

Matt ordered a whiskey sour, and the waitress left us alone again.

I glanced around, taking in the ambience and trying to avoid seeing the other couples nearby, who were holding hands or murmuring softly to each other. There was no denying the romance of the place, and it made me all the more uneasy that Matt had brought me here.

He was watching me, I realized. Shifting in my chair, I clutched for something to say, some safe topic of conversation.

"The bed and breakfast is really coming along." There, that was a good start, bringing up our mutual interest in the business of Crystal Cove and the project spearheaded by my late husband.

"Yeah, I saw Logan out there today. I guess he was checking up on stuff."

I frowned. "Logan was at the site today? That's strange, he almost always comes by after he's been there, to catch me up on how it's going."

Matt shrugged. "Maybe he was running behind today."

"Maybe."

The waitress returned with our drinks and appetizer. The

head of garlic sat in the middle of a round red plate. The ends had been cut off before it was roasted, and the aroma made my mouth water. I pulled off a slice of the crisp wheat bread, captured a clove of garlic and spread it. It was still hot and felt like heaven in my mouth.

Matt helped himself to a piece, too, and swirled his drink before taking a swig. I watched his hands, so different from Daniel's. Matt had a perpetual tan, and that included his hands. In the dim light, I could barely make out the dusting of blond hairs on the backs of his fingers.

All in all, I had to concede, Matt was a good-looking guy. I caught a few other women in the dining room sneaking peeks at him. He looked a good ten years younger than he was. His athletic lifestyle and frenetic pace kept him in shape. But I thought the real attraction was the kindness in his soft blue eyes.

The black shirt set off his blond hair. The sleeves were snug enough that I could see the muscles in his arms ripple as he reached for another slice of bread.

"I think it's going to bring a lot more business to the Cove, even to Beach Street."

Absorbed in my study of him, I was just briefly lost by what Matt said. Then I remembered and picked up the thread of conversation, grateful for something to do.

"Without a doubt. That's why Daniel and Logan decided to go that route. At first, they were thinking restaurant. Not anything to compete with the Tide, of course. I'd have wiped the floor with them, anyway, if they had gone that way. More upscale, more a fancy-dinner night place." I waved my hand, indicating the room. "Kind of like this, I guess."

"The B-and-B will attract more business. More people staying right there in town and spending their money there, rather than taking a room at the chain hotel off the highway. It's going to be good. I had the organizer of a surfing event call that woman who's managing for you guys. She booked rooms for a week next February."

I smiled. "Thanks, Matt. I don't know what Crystal Cove would do without you. You're like our business rep these days. I hope people appreciate it."

Matt ducked his head in that way I remembered from back when he was in middle school. "It's no big deal. The town is part of my family. Everyone's been there for me, supported me. It's nice to be able to return the favor."

I squeezed another piece of garlic onto my bread. This stuff was seriously good. I took a bite, chewed and swallowed before asking Matt another question.

"Do you ever think back and wish you'd done anything different, Matt? Maybe loved the Cove a little less?"

Matt chuckled and leaned back in his chair. "You're talking about Renee, right? Nah." He shook his head. "No regrets. Except maybe that we both should have been clearer from the beginning about what we wanted. I thought she wanted to stay here, help me with the store, have some kids. She thought I'd eventually get tired of this life and be willing to move somewhere else. We were both really, really wrong."

I reached across the table and squeezed his hand before snagging another piece of bread. "Do you ever hear from her?"

"Not for a long time. She lived in New York for a while, and then she moved to southern California. Got remarried about five years ago, had a baby. Birth announcement was the last thing I got."

"Does it still hurt?" I thought for a moment about how it would have felt if Daniel had chosen to leave me behind, instead of being taken away against his will. I imagined pain and betrayal.

Matt looked over my shoulder, considering, and his eyes grew distant. "Sometimes I think about what could have been. Renee and I weren't cut out for the long haul, I know that. But I would have liked kids, I think. Yours are pretty cool."

"Yeah, I like them most of the time. Truthfully, I couldn't have made it through these last few years without them."

"Well, I hope they're up for taking care of Uncle Matt in his old age. My sisters' kids are going to have their hands full with their own parents."

The waitress finally returned to take our entrée orders. I went with a penne and cream sauce, and Matt ordered veal piccata.

Sipping my wine, I studied him across the table. He was still uncomfortable about something, I could tell.

"Have you ever thought about getting married again?" My words were more abrupt than I had intended, but Matt's reaction surprised me. His face turned red, and he choked on his drink.

"Sorry," he sputtered, wiping his face with the white linen napkin. "Went down the wrong pipe."

"The idea of getting married again is that scary?" I laughed and shook my head. "Typical Matty."

"Hey, that's not fair. I liked being married. I date enough, and if someone came along who I could trust, who I could see building a life with. . .hell, yeah. I'd dive in without another thought."

"You should find a younger woman. One who still wants to have children. It's not too late for you, Matt. You'd make a great daddy."

He looked down, and I sensed I'd touched a nerve. I drained her wine glass and gave him a minute to recoup before I changed the subject.

We stuck to the comfortable topics of Crystal Cove gossip and politics all during the entrée. Matt knew everyone in the Cove, from the elderly lady who lived in one of the tiny original houses in town—I suspected Matt helped pay her taxes—to the United States congressman who had just bought a beach-front condo.

"He loves the Cove, and it wouldn't hurt to have someone in our corner with all the encroaching development." Matt leaned forward, keeping his voice low. "So I take him to lunch now and then, give his boy a free surf lesson. He's a nice guy. Doesn't hurt to have friends in high places, right?"

I took one last bite of my penne. "You amaze me. I mean, I know all you guys love this town. Daniel used to tell me sometimes the stuff you did, helping people get businesses off the ground, making sure no one was hungry or without air conditioning during the summer. But I think you're probably the most passionate about it. I'm proud of you, Matt."

His eyes were glued to the table. "That means a lot. Daniel used to say no one can build up a man like Jude. He said he never would have done half what he did if you weren't there cheering him on."

I hadn't really cried in weeks, but sitting here, hearing his words quoted to me, I missed my husband with a new keenness. I fought back the tears and instead grinned at Matt.

"Does that translate as I nagged the hell out of him until he got it done? Probably closer to the truth."

Matt shook his head. "Never. Daniel didn't ever say anything but good stuff about you. Made the rest of us hate him, sometimes. He was always the first one to go home at night, because he had someone worth going home *to*."

The waitress returned along with a busboy who cleared their plates. "Coffee? And may I bring our dessert tray? We have a delicious tiramisu tonight."

Matt looked at me with raised brows, but I just laughed, holding my stomach. "It sounds great, and I wish I could, but I'm so stuffed. Plus, I need to get home. Four AM is going to come early tomorrow."

I sat back in my chair, studying Matt as he took the check, glanced at it and then handed it back to our server along with his credit card. I hadn't been lying earlier when I'd told him he should get married again. And I could see him with a younger woman, one who would be willing to start a family. I only hoped someone would come along who could appreciate him.

"Are you sure I can't pay for my own? Or at least leave the tip?"

Matt looked wounded. "What kind of guy do you think I am? No, thanks. I take a lady out, I pay. I'm just old-fashioned that way, I guess."

The ride home was relaxed and quiet. Matt showed off the Corvette's state-of-the-art audio system as Prince crooned about purple rain. I leaned my head back against the seat and ran through the list of unattached women I knew. There weren't that many, and none I could imagine settling down with Matt.

The 'Vette purred into my driveway, and Matt turned off the ignition before he hopped out and came around to open my door. He trailed behind me as I walked toward the back door.

"Matt, you don't have to walk me to the door. I'm fine. I come home by myself pretty much all the time, you know."

Matt held the screen door while I worked the lock. "Will you stop? I'm seeing you home safe. Just like my dad always told me."

I laughed, shaking my head as I turned the knob. "Okay, well, mission accomplished. I'm inside, and all is well. I'd invite you in, but I really do have to get to bed. I'm sorry, I guess I'm not very fun these days."

"Don't apologize. It's not every night I get to have dinner with a beautiful, fascinating woman." His eyes fastened on mine, and once again I felt that thin line of dread from earlier in the evening.

"Well, clearly being fascinating is also exhausting, because I need my sleep." I tiptoed up and gave him a kiss on the cheek. Matt caught my arm, and for a moment, my heart pounded.

Then he released me, patted my back and smiled.

"Thanks for the nice evening, Jude. See you around."

Chapter Five

Logan

OVER THE PAST MONTHS—ACTUALLY, I realized it had been more than a year now—stopping in at the Rip Tide in the early morning had become part of my routine. I had always been an occasional jogger, running sporadically a few times a week, but for the last eighteen months or so, I'd been at it just about every day. Seeing Jude first thing in the morning was worth missing an hour of sleep and walking around with sore muscles.

As I made my way down the beach, my footfalls echoed against the dunes between the crashing of the waves. There was something nearly mystical about the surf at this time of day, before the sun rose and while a few last stars still twinkled in the black velvet of the sky. I could almost imagine that I was alone in the world.

I followed the bend and caught sight of Tide, nestled just beyond the edge of the sand. As I drew closer, I saw a figure silhouetted by the door. She paused, glancing over her shoulder, and I dared to hope that she was looking for me.

I turned up the narrow walkway that led to the Rip Tide. Jude raised a hand in greeting.

"Hey. You here to mooch off my water and coffee again?" It had become her standard teasing greeting.

"I'm doing you a service, testing that stuff you call coffee before you unleash it on the unsuspecting public. You ought to be paying me."

Laughing, she swung open the door. "Well, when you put it that way. . ."

I tracked her routine movements and snuck behind the bar to snag a water bottle before taking up my usual seat on a bar stool.

"So. . .you make out okay last night?"

The look Jude flashed me was a mix of guilt and worry, and my heart plummeted.

"Last night? What do you mean?"

I chose my words carefully. "Your first night without the kids. I know they went back to school yesterday. So I thought things might have felt a little. . .quiet."

"Oh." She shook her head, and I definitely detected relief. "Yeah. I was fine." She paused for a minute, measuring coffee into the machine. "Actually, I had dinner with Matt. I think he was thinking the same thing—that I might be lonely. So he took me out."

I already knew about their date, but I feigned surprise. "That was nice. Where'd you go?"

Jude shrugged. "The new Italian place. It wasn't bad. Maybe a little pretentious. But you know, restaurants. . ."

I nodded, well aware that for Jude, running a restaurant meant that eating out had lost some of its luster long ago. "Yeah. But it must've been good to get out. Have a little fun."

She smiled. "It was. Matty's a good guy, you know? He just needs. . ." Her voice trailed off, and her mouth dropped open a little as she stared out the dark window.

I frowned and followed the direction of her gaze, but I didn't see anything. "What? Jude, are you okay?"

"Hmm? Oh, yeah." She grinned across at me, and her eyes sparkled. My heart skipped a beat again, but this time for a completely different reason.

"I've been thinking and thinking since last night. Matt needs someone in his life. You know? Someone to love. Someone to love him, to take care of him. He takes care of everyone else, the town—even me. That was what last night was about. He was worried about me being alone, so he made sure to spend the evening with me. That was sweet."

"Okay." I was cautious, not sure where she was going with this.

"So it just hit me. There's this woman I met when I was doing the grief support group. You remember that? Right after Daniel died. She was actually from the Cove originally, but she's living across the bridge now. She was younger than us. I think she graduated with Molly." Matt's youngest sister was six years younger than the rest of us.

"And you think she and Matt would be good together?"

Jude put her hand on her hip and leaned against the

counter. "I think they would be freaking awesome together. Sandra is a firecracker. She's got one little girl, and she wants more kids—I remember she said that at one of the meetings. Perfect."

I propped one elbow up on the bar. "Did you and Matt talk about this last night? I thought—"

Jude glanced at me as she poured my coffee. "You thought what?"

"That maybe last night—when you said Matt took you out to dinner, I thought maybe it was more like. . .a date situation."

She stared at me for a solid moment, stopped in the middle of handing me the mug of coffee.

"A date? Matt and me? Why on earth would you think that?"

I tried to play it cool. "You said he took you out to dinner. You're single, he's single. . .why would it be so crazy for me to think it might be a date?"

She plunked down my coffee hard enough that some of it sloshed out onto the bar top.

"Um, because it's *Matt*. And *me*. We've known each other since we were in grade school."

"You knew Daniel that long, too."

Jude shook her head. "That's not the same thing."

"Why not?"

"I don't know! But it's not. Because we grew up together, maybe. Or. . .I don't know." She stalked over to the grill and flipped it on.

"Calm down. I was just asking. I'm not suggesting you and Matt are going to run off together or something. Geez."

She rolled her eyes at me as she took pancake batter and a huge carton of eggs out of the large fridge. "He's my friend. Just like you all are. I'm not stupid, Logan. I know you all—the whole posse—probably cooked up some 'let's take care of Jude' plan." She buttered the grill and whipped at the batter.

I swallowed hard. She was coming dangerously close to the truth of what the posse was doing, and I didn't want her to be hurt or offended. And I definitely didn't want her to blow my own plans out of the water, not this early in the game.

I saw her glance my way, and her gaze softened. "Logan, it's okay. I'm not mad about it. I know you all promised Daniel that you'd take care of the kids and me, and I think it's sweet." She dispensed a row of perfectly matched pancakes on the sizzling grill before walking over to cover my hand with her own.

"I appreciate it. I'm grateful for Matt taking me out last night. It did keep my mind off the kids being gone, even though I didn't know I was going to need that. I'm grateful that you're here every morning, making sure I'm okay." She patted my hand and moved back to flip the pancakes. "But I don't want you guys to treat me like I'm made of glass. I'm still Jude, the same pain in the ass you've known for years. Don't forget that."

I laughed and stood up, draining my mug. "No chance of us forgetting that. Okay, I'm out of here. Thanks for the water and the coffee."

Jude grinned. "Don't forget the scintillating conversation and fascinating company. That's on the house."

I chucked my empty water bottle into a nearby recycling container and quirked an eyebrow. "You know what, Jude? You were right. You are a pain in the ass." I started toward the door, and then swung back to shoot her a smile.

"But I kind of like it."

I left her staring after me and walked whistling back onto the beach where the first pink rays of the sun were just visible over the horizon.

Yeah, it was going to be a good day after all.

Chapter Six

Jude

I HAD A PLAN, AND I wasn't going to wait to put it into action.

As soon as the lunch rush ended, I stepped outside with my cell phone and scrolled down a list of contacts. And within minutes, I'd invited Sandra to an impromptu dinner the next day.

"We close at five on Sundays. We used to have a family dinner that day every week, but now. . ." I let my voice trail off, with just a hint of nostalgia that didn't delve into self-pity. "So I thought, what the hell! I'll just invite people over to hang out at the Tide on Sunday night. It won't be fancy, but I hope it'll be fun."

"That sounds terrific!" Sandra and her late husband had lived in South Carolina for a long time, and a hint of it remained in her voice. "What can I bring?"

I was smart enough to know that asking a guest to bring something ensured her attendance. So even though I didn't really need it, I said, "Would you bring some kind of dessert? We'll have dinner covered here."

"Definitely! Is it all right for me bring Lily with me? I could leave her with my folks, but I try not to abuse their generosity."

"Of course, I expected that you would. My nieces will be here, too, I hope, and my friends Eric and Janet have two boys. A little older than Lily, but you know kids. They'll all hang out together."

"Oh, thanks, Jude. I really appreciate you thinking of me. It's like a godsend. I've been a little lonely lately. I'll see you at five tomorrow."

"Looking forward to it!" I clicked off with a broad smile. Matchmaking had never been my thing, but maybe it was going to be part of this new phase in my life. I'd be the old lady in town who everyone went to when they were looking for love. It might be fun. It might take my mind off missing my own one true love.

I gave my head a little shake. This wasn't about me, and it was damned nice to think about doing something for others after I'd spent the last few years leaning into my friends and family. I never took their generosity of time and attention for granted, but it was good to be on the other end of the equation.

Now I had Sandra set for tomorrow. I just needed to make sure Matt would be here, too. The easiest way to do that was to make this into a big group gathering. Matty never missed one of those.

Inviting the posse was a simple matter of one call to my sister-in-law, Samantha. The informal phone tree that was in place for all events or emergencies sprang into action, and by the time

Emmy showed up at five to relieve me, Sam had called back to report that everyone was coming to my Sunday night shin-dig.

"Emmy, why don't you come, too?" I leaned against the counter. I'd just detailed my plan to the night manager. "Bring the kids. It'll be fun."

"Come back here on my off hours? Are you nuts?" Emmy shook her head and laughed. "Okay, sure. But only because my children would kill me if I said no to an evening of fried foods and playing with other kids. Want me to bring a pie?"

"Nah, like you said, it's your day off. Plus, I asked Sandra to bring dessert. Just bring yourself and the kids."

"Done." Emmy grinned. "So who's going to cook?"

"Everyone. I'll try to make extras of everything through-out the day, and then I'll draft some of the guys into manning the grill. It'll be casual, but we'll be having fun."

"Awesome. Now tell me why you're really doing this."

I widened my eyes. "What do you mean? I have to have an ulterior motive for dinner with my friends?"

"Of course not, but you have a gleam in your eye. You're up to something."

Shrugging, I winked. "Watch and learn, my young appren-tice. Watch and learn."

The Rip Tide was hopping for a Sunday. I felt like I needed roller skates to keep up with the rush, even with Sadie and Mack working alongside me. The clear blue skies and bright sun had people flocking to the beach, and it seemed everyone had decided to enjoy a late lunch before heading home to start another week.

"Three burgers, fried chicken and a salad for number eighteen." Sadie stomped back into our open kitchen. "Plus, those kids at the bar want two more orders of fries and refills on drinks." She clipped the ticket to the rack, as Mack squinted up at it.

"Good God, woman, your chicken scratch gets worse every day."

Sadie scowled and slammed the basket into the fryer. "I just told you what the order was. And it's not my writing, *old man*. It's your eyes and those glasses you won't go get updated."

I rolled my eyes. I'd been the buffer here for so long that it came naturally to me now. The busier the restaurant was, the worse the older couple became. I grabbed three beef patties from my stock in the fridge and set them down next to Mack at the grill.

"I'll handle the salad and the chicken." I read the ticket and bit the side of my lip, determined to be as diplomatic as possible. "Sadie, is this. . .chicken Caesar salad?"

"No." Sadie tore the paper from my hand. "Right here, see? Chicken ranch." She clipped it back on the rack and went back to her fries, a frown still on her face. At the grill, Mack made the mistake of snickering.

Sadie wheeled around, snatched up a large metal spoon from the nearby jar and shook it at Mack. "You keep it up! Don't think I won't take this to you. Right upside the head. And no one would blame me a bit. No court in the land would convict me, not for what I put up with from you!"

I clamped down on the insides of my cheeks to keep from laughing, knowing the old woman wouldn't hesitate to turn that spoon on me next.

"Sadie, here." I handed her a bowl with breaded chicken tenders. "Put these in the fryer, please. And give me the spoon. We don't have time today to clean up the mess if you decide to beat Mack senseless."

Sadie humphed, but she pulled out tongs and dropped the chicken pieces into the bubbling oil. Over her head, I exchanged a glance with Mack before we all got back to work.

I wasn't usually strict about closing time on Sundays, and often we had stragglers for an hour beyond five. But today, I turned over the 'closed' sign at four-thirty. By the time Janet walked in at five, the last customer was just cashing out.

I chased Mack and Sadie out of the kitchen, forcing icy beers on both of them. When my sister-in-law came back behind the bar for a hug, she wrinkled her nose.

"Was it a long day? You like you were ridden hard and put away wet."

"Thanks, love you, too." I rolled my shoulders. "Busy, and Mack and Sadie were at each other like they do when we get slammed. It'll be okay. But can you keep your eye on things for five minutes? I brought a change of clothes, and I want to run upstairs and put them on before we get started."

"Sure. I'm going to pour myself a drink, that okay?"

I untied my apron and tossed it in the barrel by the back door as I headed toward the staircase. "Absolutely. Pour me one, too, and make it a double, please."

The apartment over the restaurant was tiny. When Daniel

and I had moved in after our wedding, it had been romantic and fun, finding used furniture, using mismatched dishes and pots and pans handed down from our families. Close quarters hadn't been a problem. And even after Meggie was born, she had taken up so little space, and it had been handy to leave her sleeping upstairs in her crib while I worked in the restaurant, baby monitor hooked to my belt.

Since we moved, the apartment was more of a flophouse, I thought as I stripped off my shorts and T-shirt in the miniscule bathroom. It was a handy place to crash when the posse hung at the Tide and maybe had a little too much to drink. The kids used it sporadically during their summers at home, too, especially when their friends came to visit.

I had considered selling the house and moving back here, right after Daniel died. The kids and my brother Mark had talked me out of it, arguing that if I did that, I'd never get a break from work. They probably had a point.

I gave into the temptation of a quick shower now, knowing my sister-in-law and friends were more than capable of running the show on their own for a few extra minutes. And it felt heavenly to let the water sluice over me, to feel the grease and stress of the day slide down the drain.

Dressed again in a fresh shorts and a thin cotton tank top, I sprinted down the steps and ran smack into Logan.

I'd seen him this morning, of course, as I had opened up, but tonight he too was freshly showered, dressed in jeans and a white polo shirt that brought out his deep tan. His light brown hair was damp as it fell across his forehead, skimming his dark eyes.

He grabbed my arm to steady me. "Whoa, there. Where's the fire?"

I felt that same disturbing skitter in my heartbeat that had been showing up whenever I saw him lately.

Logan, I reminded myself. *This is just Logan, one of my best friends.*

"The fire better be in my kitchen, under some burgers." To prove to myself that I could be casual with him, that my feelings weren't changing into something alarming, I stood on tiptoe and kissed Logan's cheek. "Glad you're here. Ready to see my plan spring into action?"

Logan released my arm, frowning. I wondered if I'd upset him with the kiss.

"Seeing as neither of the necessary parties are here yet, I think I have a little while before show time."

Now it was my brow that furrowed. "Matt's not here yet? Or Sandra? Are you sure? I told them both five." I scanned the room. "It's twenty after."

Logan shrugged. "I heard there was traffic on the bridge. Maybe that hung up your friend." His eyes lingered on my damp hair, wandered down my neck, making me acutely aware of the small rise of my breasts visible at the top of the tank.

I shook my head to clear it. "Did you get a drink yet? Sam's supposed to be making one for me." I didn't wait for an answer but turned to head for the bar.

Samantha and Janet were busy in the kitchen, pulling condiments from the fridge and setting up baskets of buns. Emmy was fiddling with the stereo, trying to queue up some music.

"None of your country twang, Em!" I gave her a friendly nudge. "Play something cool."

Emmy didn't look up. "Oh, you mean like Billy Idol? Adam Ant?"

"They would definitely meet the cool requirement, but since your taste in music is still, umm. . ." I cocked my head, considering. ". . .maturing, I'll compromise on Pat Benatar."

"That's a compromise?" Emmy sighed. "I have a great mix list. I promise, you'll be happy with it. I even have some Blondie."

"I guess I'll trust you. Any love songs on there? We might need them later." I winked and went in search of the drink my sister-in-law had promised.

"Captain and coke waiting for you in the back, Jude!" Sam called.

"You're my favorite sister-in-law, you know that?" I found the glass and took a long swig. Spying my brother flipping burgers, I made my way to his side.

"Hey, trouble." He reached around my shoulders to give me a quick squeeze. "Look at this, you got me back at my old job."

I grinned. "Yeah, and any time you get tired of training the young minds of tomorrow, feel free to come back. We can always use another hand at the grill." I glanced over my shoulder and lowered my voice. "One of these days, Sadie really is going to beat Mack. Or maybe pick up a knife instead of a spoon. Came real close today."

Mark winced. "I don't miss that. I remember when I was a kid thinking they were ancient and worrying one of them was going to drop dead, yelling at the other. Dad used to just laugh."

"Every time I hint at retirement, Sadie blows a gasket and

Mack begs me not to make them stay home together. And truthfully, I don't know I could run this place without them. The thought of having to train someone to do what they do gives me hives." I reached around and pulled a too-hot fry out of the basket.

"So you doing okay, sis?" Mark kept his eyes trained on the burger he was getting ready to flip, but I knew he could do it in his sleep. I punched his shoulder.

"Yes, I'm fine. Logan checks on me every morning, and Matt took me to dinner Friday night. Sam and/or Janet call me every day. I'm feeling the love, but please stop worrying."

Mark moved the burger onto the plate next to the grill and smiled. "Whatever you say. Hey, can you grab me some cheese for this next batch?"

I turned toward the fridge just as the door to the restaurant opened. Sandra came in, looking more than a little worse for the wear, followed by a little girl in pigtails who I assumed was her daughter, Lily. Holding the door and bringing up the rear was Matt.

"Here, Mark." I tossed the block of Swiss in my brother's direction and went to greet the newcomers.

"I'm so sorry we're late!" Sandra hugged me and then held me at arms' length. "And I'm a mess! My car broke down on the inter-coastal bridge, and I was standing out there in the heat. . ." Her eyes slid sideways. "Until my hero showed up."

Sandra's dimpled smile turned full force on Matt, who flushed and managed to look both uncomfortable and pleased at the same time.

"Matt! You rescued Sandra and Lily?"

He shook his head, grinning all the while. "I just stopped to help. Anyone would have done the same."

"But no one else did except you." Sandra laid one hand on his arm and smiled before she turned back to me. "I'd called for the road rescue, but they said they were going to be over an hour coming. Matt here put flares around my car, took Lily and me into his air-conditioned Jeep and convinced the tow truck to come sooner. He was amazing."

"That's our Matt," I murmured, meeting Logan's eyes across the room. "Always a hero." I stifled the urge to do a victory dance. "Let's get you all something to drink and some food. You must be famished." I smiled at the little girl. "Lily, the kids are all eating out of the deck, so they can run back and forth onto the beach. Why don't you go out with them?"

I maneuvered Matt and Sandra to a two-person table away from all the noise of the kitchen and went in search of drinks for them. As I bent to grab a beer for Matt, I felt a hand at my waist and knew it was Logan.

"You couldn't have set that up better if you'd tried," he murmured into my ear. I shivered and caught my breath before I pulled myself together enough to turn and smile.

"Funny how things work out sometimes, isn't it?"

"If I didn't know better, I'd think you messed with her car and made sure Matt was coming from the same direction." He narrowed his eyes. "You didn't, right?"

I rolled my eyes. "Right. God, Logan, what do you think of me?"

He grinned down at me. "Wouldn't you like to know?"

Before I could answer, Mark slid a basket of onion rings onto the counter in front of me.

"Can you take these over to Cooper and Eric? I promised them a hot batch."

"Sure." I spied the guys at a table in the corner, tipping back bottles. Sparring Logan one last glance, I picked up the food.

"Onion rings to the dudes who clearly aren't looking to get lucky tonight." I dropped the basket between them.

"Hey, don't make assumptions. I'm going to take a few of these over to Janet. If she eats them, too, she won't be able to tell the difference." Eric winked at me and sauntered over to the bar where his wife was slicing hamburger buns.

I took his empty chair and pushed the basket closer to Cooper. "What about you, stud? Don't you want to keep your options open for the evening?"

He quirked a grin at me. "No options tonight. Lex is with me." He jerked a thumb in the direction of the deck. "She's outside riding herd on the rug rats. Pretending to be annoyed, but she secretly loves it."

I glanced out the doors. Alexis was leaning against the deck railing, her eyes trained on the beach below, where Mark's kids were playing. Her red hair was twisted into a braid that trailed down her back.

"How's she doing? Ready to start high school?"

Cooper winced. "Don't remind me. I tried to talk Jolie into sending to her to an all-girl Catholic school."

I laughed. Cooper and his first ex-wife were one of those rare couples whose divorce was far friendlier than their marriage had ever been. Alexis was a happy and well-adjusted girl because her parents worked together to raise her.

"Good luck with that. You might as well face it, Coop. You're going to be beating the boys off with a stick. I don't want to scare you, but when Lex was working for me this summer, there were plenty of them looking at her. Don't worry, I kept my eye on her—and them."

Cooper leaned back in his chair, closing his eyes. "I'm choosing to live in a blissful state of denial. She's still my little girl."

I laid my hand on his arm. "You keep telling yourself that. Don't worry. She's a good girl. I loved having her around here. Meggie did, too. She says Lex is the closest thing she has to a little sister."

"I'm glad. I really did appreciate you letting her work for you. It was a good way to get her feet wet, and I knew you were looking out for her." Cooper covered my hand with his free one and held it for just a second longer than necessary.

I smiled to cover my sudden discomfort and stood up. "If I don't get back to cooking, my brother is going to kill me. I think he's afraid if he gets behind the bar too long, he'll end up never leaving. It's a family thing."

"Jude."

I turned back, unease rising at the intimate tone of his voice.

"This was really nice. Thanks for having all of us. Good to be together again for a happy reason."

There was a look in Cooper's eyes that I hadn't seen in a long time, and it certainly had never been directed my way. Not quite sure what to do, I nodded and got back to the kitchen as fast as my stumbling feet could carry me.

But even as I scurried back to the grill, I felt more than one pair of eyes watching me. Across the room, nursing his beer, Logan watched me and frowned.

Chapter Seven

Logan

I SAT AT MY DESK IN the room I'd designed expressly for the purpose of designing from home. I had an office across the bridge in Elson, where I met clients and from which the day-to-day running of Holt/Hawthorne was accomplished. But I preferred to do my creative work here.

The room was almost entirely windows, placed intentionally so that I had the best light at almost any point in the day. My drafting table faced the beach, because I had always drawn inspiration from the mercurial surf. I was a beach kid, after all; I might not have embraced my inner surfer like Matt had, but it was no less in my blood. I simply preferred to take the moods of the ocean and translate them into homes that complemented rather than scarred the landscape.

Home was important to me, had been since my own family had disintegrated when I was just thirteen years old. I didn't talk about it, didn't even think about it most of the time, but I knew my mother's departure and my parents' messy divorce were what had motivated me to build a house that was far too large for a man living by myself, as well as what drove me to design homes for others.

I'd never experienced any kind of creative block, not really. Daniel used to kid me about being the temperamental artist half of our duo, while he himself was the muscle, but we both knew that it was joke. When a plan had to be drawn up, I did it. I didn't have to wait for a muse. It was already within me.

But tonight. . .I tossed down the pencil and stretched my neck. Thanks to the regularity of my morning jogging, I wasn't sore anymore. But the tension in my shoulders was another story, and I knew the source.

Jude.

When we'd sat in here in my bar over a month ago, and made that deal, I hadn't been worried. I knew Jude, knew she wasn't going to jump at the first chance for a new relationship. But getting everyone on board meant that when I was finally ready to make my own move, I'd do it with the full support of my friends. No one could get mad at me when I'd already gotten pre-approval from the posse.

I rubbed a hand over my face. That comfortable feeling had lasted just until the day I had spied Matt walking out of the Tide in the middle of the afternoon. Not that it was unusual; we all worked in such close proximity that not dropping in on the others would have been odder. But I had a gut-deep feeling that day. I had planned to stick my head in at the Tide and say hello to Jude, let her know how the bed and breakfast was progressing, but it felt too much like one-upmanship after seeing Matt.

So instead I had followed up with a phone call to Matt on my way back to the office. I made small talk and then an off-the-cuff suggestion that we grab a beer and some steaks at my house that night, like we did on so many other evenings.

"Uh, actually. . ." Matt had replied slowly, and I had my answer. "I'm taking Jude out to eat. Her kids went left today, so I thought. . ."

"You thought you'd make your move." I had not intended for the words to come out so harsh.

"It's not like that." I could almost picture Matt running his hand over the shaggy blond hair. "I'm trying to do what we said. Hell, I paced around the shop today for an hour, trying to make up my mind to go and do it. Ask her. I mean, it's Jude. I tried to figure out, do I think about her that way? Could I be with her? One part of me says no. She's like one of my sisters, for God's sake. But then another part says, maybe. Maybe we could be comfortable together. You know, grow old."

I nearly drove off the road. One word I never associated with Jude was comfortable. And growing old? Yeah, eventually, but we were a long way from that yet.

"You gotta be sure, Matt," I had said aloud. "Think about it." When my friend didn't respond, I added, "Have a good time tonight. Catch you later."

Now, standing at the window, watching the swirl of twilight waves, I pondered my next move. The early morning jogs and stops at the Tide had been part of the groundwork I was laying, sure, but it was also feeding a need I had just to be around Jude, to talk with her. I had been reassured when she reported on her dinner with Matt, even more so when she fixed him up with her friend, but on the other hand, she had been shocked at the idea of having a dating relationship with Matt.

Was it because of Matt himself, or was she not interested in anyone at all? I couldn't be sure. When she had nearly fallen into my arms at the Tide the night of her matchmaker dinner, I had lost my breath. Her dark hair damp, falling around her shoulders in tendrils as she ran down the steps, had taken me back years to when we'd all hung out there during the summers, none of us bothering to change out of bathing suits, our hair perpetually wet from the last dip in the ocean.

And just before she kissed my cheek, I almost thought I had seen something in her eyes. . .I shook my head. Sooner or later, I would have to do something more than just hang around her. Matt might be out of the picture now—Jude had gleefully reported that he and Sandra had seen each other almost every night of the past two weeks since their meeting—but there was still Cooper.

Cooper with two marriages under his belt, and a teenaged daughter Jude had taken under her wing. That would be an in for him. Cooper, who, at Jude's matchmaking dinner, had said something that flustered her, had her blushing.

I sighed and sank into the chair that sat by my drafting table. Yeah, it was getting to be time to make my move.

Only I wasn't exactly sure what that move was.

Chapter Eight

Jude

AFTER DANIEL DIED, I HAD worried a little about being lonely. I had pictured long empty evenings, nights in front of the television, solitary meals at a silent kitchen table.

But so far, that had not materialized. In fact, I was so surrounded by company and activity that it was beginning to wear on my nerves. I didn't like turning people down, so I agreed to an afternoon of shopping in Daytona with Janet. And then an evening at some author's reading at a nearby independent bookstore with Samantha. Dinner with Matt and Sandra, who insisted that I had brought them together, and they wanted to thank me.

Between my friends padding my social calendar, my kids calling to check on me, and the normal hustle and bustle of the Rip Tide, I didn't have a moment to hear myself think.

So on Thursday night, I convinced Mack and Sadie to go home before I locked up by telling them I was staying in town for a little while for a business meeting. As much as I hated lying to anyone, especially to the couple who had been like second parents to me, I knew it was the only ploy that would work. If I told them that I was planning to stay late to give the kitchen a deep cleaning, they would insist on staying with me the whole time.

Once I watched them drive away, I let out a long sigh of relief. I had already turned the sign to 'Closed' and switched on the outside lights, as though I was leaving. From the back room, I pulled out a basket of rags, a mop, bucket and a tote full of cleaning products.

"How sad am I?" I muttered, half-amused and half-horrified that the prospect of an evening of cleaning was making me nearly giddy.

I changed the radio station to the weekly '80s flashback show, cranked up the volume, pulled on rubber gloves and launched a full-force attack on the grill.

Logan

I liked routine, and his hadn't changed much in the years since I'd built my beach house. I left the office and drove over the bridge to come home. Twice a week, I stopped at the grocery store to buy food for dinners. On Mondays, I left early enough to pick up my dry cleaning and pressed shirts before the cleaners closed. Occasionally, if I was invited to a friend's house for dinner or if I had another social engagement, the routine could vary. But most weeks, it didn't.

After Daniel got sick, I had changed up things a little. Once I crossed the bridge, I cut down two side streets so that I could drive past Jude and Daniel's house to make sure everything was all right. Just seeing the lights on in the right places was somehow comforting. On the days when the lights weren't on, I'd know something had come up, and more likely than not, Daniel was in the hospital. Again.

Now, of course, no movement in the house just meant that Jude was out, and most of the time, I knew where she was. The posse was close enough that word traveled fast, and it wasn't unusual for Mark or Eric to let slip if one of their wives had plans with Jude, or if something else happened to be going on.

The house pass was followed by a detour that led me to Beach Street, where I checked out the Rip Tide. On weeknights, the parking lot was usually empty, with only the security lights still burning. Fridays were a different, of course, but I still made certain that Jude's car had vacated its normal spot, meaning that Emmy had taken over. Since Jude typically followed her own routine, it was reassuring to me on a very basic level to know that she was safe.

So when I drove past her house that Thursday, I was only a little surprised to see just one light in the kitchen. I assumed her car was safely in the garage where it belonged, and that Jude herself was probably there in the kitchen.

But as I made the pass by the Tide, I frowned. Jude's car was still in the lot, and I could see lights throughout the restaurant, as if it were still open. I pulled in and parked next to her beat-up compact—though Daniel had tried to convince her to buy a newer model, Jude claimed it was pointless to have a new car when she lived at the beach.

I saw the 'Closed' sign on the door as I approached, but then I heard something. I cocked my head. It sounded like. . .drums. Loud drums. And a woman's voice.

I tried the door handle. I wasn't surprised that it was unlocked; Jude was notorious for not locking doors. As I stepped into the empty restaurant, the music assaulted my senses. The drums pounded in my chest, and my ears rang.

Across the room, I spied Jude. She hadn't heard me come in, and no wonder. I took advantage of the chance to watch her, unseen.

Her hair was up in its typical ponytail, and it swung in time with her movements. She was wearing jean shorts and a deep green T-shirt, with the rounded neckline she usually favored. She swung her hips and arms in time to the drums. And she was singing at the top of her lungs along with Sheila E.

I was transfixed, watching her denim-covered rear wiggle and gyrate. The shirt had ridden up a little on her back, and I could see a small slice of tanned skin. My fingers itched to touch it, and I clenched my fist to keep from reaching out, as if, somehow, I could from this distance.

As she spun and shimmied, I was suddenly back in high school, standing down at the old pavilion where the summer dances were held. Every Saturday night, the whole posse met at the Rip Tide and walked down the beach toward the sound of the music. A different business sponsored the dance each week, so we never knew what the decorations would be: one Saturday it might be sea shells and shimmery green bunting, while another there might be album covers and ads from the local record store.

Regardless, the dances drew most of the teens in the Cove. Everyone brought blankets, and as the evening wore on, couples would drift away from the lights and music, returning some time later, often disheveled and slightly sandy. But Daniel and Jude were seldom among those, only because Jude adored dancing. She didn't want to miss even one song, and if Daniel begged off, she had no compunction about pulling another one of the posse in to join her.

Remembering, I moved toward her now, tugging loose my tie as I went. The music muffled my steps, and I might have reached her entirely undetected, except that Jude chose that moment to execute a perfect spin.

She saw me, and her hand flew to her throat. She screeched in shock, and for a moment, I thought she might pass out. I knew the minute surprise was superseded by annoyance, but before she could say anything, I stuck out one hand.

"Dance with me?"

Jude's face melted into a smile as she took my hand. I spun her once, and then simply held her hand, moving in synchronicity to her steps and swings as Sheila E. continued to tout the benefits of a glamorous life.

After a few moments, the drums gave way to the more mellow guitar of Madonna's *Crazy For You*. I pulled Jude close, wrapping my other arm around her back, just I had wanted to do over twenty years before. In those days, when the music had slowed, Jude always turned away, her eyes searching for Daniel until he found her on the dance floor.

But tonight, her wide green eyes fastened on me. For a moment, I feared she might pull away; confusion and a hint of trepidation clouded her face. Then she relaxed and rested her forehead against my shoulder, slipping her hand around to press against my back.

I wondered if she could hear the pounding of my heart. How many years had this been my dream? All through high school, definitely. Even when I had known that Jude would always love Daniel, that he would come first in her heart for the rest of their lives, I had still dreamed. I had never betrayed how I felt in any way. I had stood up for them at their wedding as Daniel's best man, offered the toast, kissed the bride on her cheek. I'd been there for first Meghan's birth and then for Joseph's arrival.

I hadn't been obsessed with Jude all those years. I had lived a full life and had had several relationships, because I knew that being in love with my best friend's one true love and wife was an untenable situation. So at some point, I had simply decided to stop.

But now here we were. Jude was in my arms, swaying with me. I could feel the heat of her breath against my chest, her fingers moving absently over my shirt, her other hand small and fragile in mine. Desire rose, and I swallowed, hard.

I knew he should leave it alone. Enjoy the dance, revel in the feel of her against me, and for now at least, leave it at that.

Almost of its own volition, my hand moved up her back, skimming over her neck. I stopped moving and laid my fingers against her cheek, pulling back so I could see her. My eyes moved down to her lips, and I tilted up her chin. I had just begun to lean down toward her when her eyes flew open, and she stepped back.

"Logan. . ." My name escaped her on a breath, but in it, I heard the rejection.

Forcing a smile, I rubbed her arm before releasing her. "Sorry. I didn't mean to startle you. I saw the lights, and I just stopped to make sure you were okay. When I saw you dancing—" I looked away. "I was thinking of the pavilion dances. Remember?"

Jude licked her lips and wrapped her arms around her stomach. I felt her discomfort, but my desire was stronger, and I had to step even farther away to lean against the counter.

"Of course, I remember them. We used to have so much fun." Jude walked to the radio and turned it down. "You must think I'm crazy, dancing in an empty restaurant by myself."

"No, but what *are* you doing here? By yourself?"

She rolled her eyes. "That was kind of the point. I haven't had very much quiet time lately, and I just wanted to be by myself. I'm cleaning the kitchen." She indicated the pile of rags on the floor.

"Well, obviously that was what you were doing when I came in." I decided a little teasing was the way to go. Shift the focus, take the pressure off Jude. It worked, and she smiled.

"Music helps me work, and I never could resist Sheila E."

"Who could?" I grinned and shook my head. "Sorry I interrupted your alone time. I'll see you later."

"Logan." I stopped at her voice and turned back.

"Would you stay a little? I've probably got another half

hour of work here. I mean, if you don't have anything better to do."

I thought of the single breast of chicken sitting in my refrigerator at home. "Nope, I got nothing. But I thought you wanted to be alone."

She shrugged. "I had some of that. Now I want some company, if that's okay."

I unbuttoned my cuffs and began rolling up my sleeves. "I'll stay if you let me help. We'll get done faster, and then I'm taking you down the street to Jimmie's for an ice cream cone. Deal?"

Jude studied me for a minute before smiling. "Deal." She tossed me a rag. "Want to do the cabinets?"

Chapter Nine

Cooper

I KNEW WOMEN.

Raised by a single mother, married twice, and now the father of a teenaged girl, I was fairly certain there wasn't too much about the female species I didn't understand. So the idea of a relationship with Jude didn't faze me at all.

I knew marriage wasn't in the cards for me, not again. I'd vowed after my failed second attempt that I wouldn't go down that road again. But the way I figured it, Jude wasn't some starry-eyed girl. She probably didn't want to get married again either. I pictured us in one of those very mature, modern relationships. We could keep our own houses, even our own lives. It would be nice to have a dependable date for things like weddings and reunions, without all the mess of marriage. And finding someone who already loved Alexis, whom Lex loved, too, was a bonus I just couldn't deny.

I was sitting in my workshop, sanding down a credenza before I stained it as I considered our options. Being a carpenter was a calling, and one I had always been content to have. All of us in the posse had been proud of Logan when he'd gone to college and become an architect, and of Daniel when he'd earned his business degree and opened his general contracting business. But the great thing about our friends was that they were no less happy for Eric when he'd became a master plumber and for me when I opened my carpentry shop.

My phone buzzed, and I grinned when I saw the caller ID. *Jude.* Well, if that wasn't just like the universe, handing me an opportunity to lay down some groundwork.

I answered, keeping my voice low yet professional. "Cooper Davis."

"Hey, Coop. It's Jude. Got a minute?"

"For you, gorgeous, more than one. What can I do for you?"

"I wanted to check with you about the piece for the bed and breakfast. The one for the foyer? We're working on nailing down the opening date, and I told Logan I'd help him with some of the loose ends."

I eased over to my messy, paper-piled desk and flipped over a page on my planner. "It's on track to be finished by the end of next week. I can have it delivered any time after that."

"Oh, that's great. I'll let them know, and one of us will get back to you about a definite date."

"Okay." I paused as inspiration struck. "You know, Jude, I'm glad you called. I was thinking about the stain for that piece, and I'd love it if you could come down here, take a look at the choices."

"Oh, sure. I can do that. Could I stop this afternoon, after we close? I could be there before six, I think, if that's not too late for you."

"That would be perfect. I'll see you then." I clicked off, ran my hand over the credenza and nodded in satisfaction.

~⚬~

Jude

I was beginning to feel as though I had fallen into an alternate reality. First it had been Matt, with the dinner that had veered dangerously close to date territory. I had convinced myself I was wrong about that, and now that he was happy with Sandra, it was easier to accept.

And then there was the weird vibe I'd been getting from Logan, culminating in our dance the other night. I knew— *knew*—he had been about to kiss me. Dancing with him had been stepping onto dangerous ground. When his arms went around me, my stomach had gone liquid with an odd feeling that had shot straight down my knees.

This was something I had heard mentioned in my grief support group: lonely widows who saw attraction or love behind every expression of support or comfort. I was determined not to be that woman. After all, it had been thirty years since I had even considered a man other than Daniel. Being out of practice was kind of a given, and the last thing I wanted to do was mistake compassion for passion.

So I had resolved to be friendly and natural with all of my friends. In the mornings when Logan stopped by, I kept our conversation light. I didn't stand too close to him, and I didn't let my imagination wander.

Not too far, anyway.

Driving to Cooper's shop after a long day at the Tide, my mind kept darting back to dancing with Logan. How he had looked at me when we were fast dancing, and then the slow melt of his eyes when the Madonna song came on. The way his arms had pulled me flush to his body, fitting me to him in a way that was both foreign and familiar at the same time.

Snap out of it, I warned myself. *It's Logan. He's just doing what he promised. Taking care of me.*

Cooper's shop was tucked away on the far edge of town, away from the beach and farther east than my house. He had bought the tiny Cape Cod dirt cheap for the spacious workshop in the backyard. Eventually, he had gutted the house, turning the dining room into his business office and the bedrooms upstairs into an apartment of sorts, a place where he could sleep when he worked late. It also became the spot where he'd crashed between marriages.

The sun was setting as I pulled into the driveway. Cooper's Jeep was still in the back, parked at angle to the rear of the workshop, and the high whirring sound of a sander came from inside.

I climbed out of the car and followed the noise. I opened the door to the workshop with caution; I knew how involved Cooper became, and startling him when he was working with a machine could have some nasty consequences.

He was at the far end of the open room, holding the massive sander in arms that bulged with the effort. Safety glasses protected his eyes, and he wore jeans and a tight white T-shirt with boots I knew were steel-toed.

Cooper was tallest of the posse. In high school, we'd called him Scarecrow until he'd begun to fill out a little, but even now, he tended toward thinness. He kept his black hair short, mostly because he said it was too hard to keep the sawdust out if it got long.

I closed the door and stood still, waiting until he saw me. Once he did, he turned off the sander and turned to put it down on a nearby shelf.

Pulling off the goggles, Cooper waved me over. "Hey! You been there long?"

I stepped carefully around the furniture in various stages of development and smiled. "No, just got here. I—" I stopped in surprise as Cooper swept me into a hug the minute I was close enough.

"Sorry, I'm covered in dust. But don't worry, it wipes off." Cooper grinned. "How was your day?"

"Umm. . ." I brushed bits of wood from my cheek. "It was good. How about you?"

He lifted one shoulder. "Not bad. Busy in here, but no client meetings, so that's always good."

I laughed. "Cooper, client meetings are how you get new business. You know you have to see people at some point."

"I do. I'm seeing you, right?"

I shook my head. "I don't count."

Cooper's mouth twisted. "I'd have to disagree." His eyes roamed over my face, and I froze for a moment, and then forced my lips into a smile.

"For someone who says he doesn't like people, you sure are a flirt."

An expression I couldn't define skittered across Cooper's face. "You don't get two ex-wives without a little flirting, I guess. I can pull 'em in, but the 'not-liking-people' deal makes it hard to hold onto them."

"I'm sorry." I touched his arm. "I didn't mean that. I was only teasing."

"Don't worry about it." He squeezed my shoulder and left his hand there as he turned them around. "That table is in the back. Come on."

Cooper had been working with Holt/Hawthorne since their first project. He did specialty jobs, things like banisters, mantles and built-in furniture. When Daniel and Logan began delving into investment properties, like the bed and breakfast, they'd increased Cooper's participation and even offered to bring him as partner. But Cooper hated the business end of the job. For him, it was all about the wood and what he found within in it.

I loved to visit his shop. To me, it was miraculous that anyone could take a few pieces of wood and turn them into functional works of art. I ran her hand over a delicate desk with spindly legs and complicated carved edges.

"This is so pretty, Cooper. Who is it for?"

He spared it a passing a glance. "Lady over in Lake Mariah. She had a desk like when she was young, but it got lost at some point, and she wants to recreate it. I made it from an old picture."

"That's amazing." I followed Cooper to a corner where a narrow table stood. One side had a straight beveled edge, while the rest of it curved into a half circle. It was designed to stand flush against the wall in the foyer and would hold baskets of information for the guests of the bed and breakfast.

"Wow. This is going to be perfect. I can just see it in the entryway."

"Yeah, I think so. So here are your stain choices. The initial order was for a chai latte stain." He held up a sample chip, laid it against the table. "But I wanted to make sure you hadn't added other furniture in that room that might not work with this shade. Lot easier to change the order now than it will be next week."

I tilted my head. "What are my other choices?"

"Gingerbread House. Hot Chocolate. Apple Cider. Maple Syrup." Cooper laid the squares on the table in a perfect row.

"Are those really the names? They're making me hungry."

Cooper shrugged. "Companies make them up. If it were me, it would be dark brown, lighter brown, reddish brown and golden brown." He glanced at me speculatively. "Did you want something to eat? I think there's some fruit in the house. Or maybe in the fridge in here."

"Nah, I'm good, thanks." I rubbed her bottom lip with one finger as I studied the stains. "I like the original choice, but you know, I bought a lamp a few months back that would be perfect for the center of this table. It's Tiffany—well, Tiffany-esque." I smiled at Cooper, who looked slightly lost.

"Anyway, the lamp is mostly red glass, and I'm thinking that maybe that—what is it, Apple Cider? That would look terrific."

Cooper nodded. "Okay. It'll be ready next week. I'll call you when we can schedule it for delivery."

"Thanks, Cooper. It's going to be gorgeous."

He nodded, looking down the sawdust-covered floor. "It was the last piece I planned with Daniel. He told me what should go there, just a few weeks before he—" Cooper's mouth worked.

I closed my hand over his. "I know. Lasts are the worst thing. If you knew all the times I've thought about it. . .last year, when I finished using the final tube of toothpaste I'd shared with Daniel, I cried for an hour." I shook my head. "Crazy, right?"

"No, not crazy." Cooper turned his hand, lacing his fingers through mine. "It means you loved him. Those things wouldn't hurt if you didn't."

"I guess."

We stood for a moment, both of us remembering. Gradually, I became aware that Cooper was still holding my hand. When I tried to gently tug it loose, he gripped it tighter.

"Jude," he whispered, pulling me closer.

I swallowed hard and licked my lips. My heart was pounding, but not in the same way it did when Logan had danced with me. Before I could say anything or step back, Cooper's arm gripped around my back, and he lowered his mouth to cover mine.

At first, all I could think was, *Cooper's kissing me!* Panic coursed through my veins, but I wasn't certain if it was because Cooper's lips were over mine. . .or if it were simply because his lips were not Daniel's.

I managed a single coherent thought—*well, why NOT Cooper?*—before his mouth opened, and I felt his tongue against my closed lips. I made the decision and opened to his persuasion.

It only took a moment for me to realize that my heart had slowed to its normal rate. I became aware of Cooper's fingers against my back, but only because he was pressing against my bra strap, and the hooks were digging into my spine. I mused that Cooper was a decent kisser, which wasn't surprising, but what did it say that I was only enjoying it, not being swept away?

I took advantage of him pulling back slightly for a breath and spoke against his mouth.

"Cooper—"

He would have gone back for seconds, but I ducked my head. "No—Cooper. Listen. Wait."

He stepped back, still holding me. "What's wrong?"

"Nothing's wrong, but Cooper—you kissed me."

He rubbed his jaw, but his eyes didn't leave my face. "I'm aware of that. I was standing right here."

"But Cooper. *Me.* You kissed *me.* What are you thinking?"

He dropped my hand and turned away a little. "I don't know. I guess I was thinking that I wanted to kiss you, so I did. I mean, Jude, you know, I always liked you. We get along. We're both, um. . .you know, not with anyone right now. So why not?"

I choked back all the why nots that flooded my mind and chose the least hurtful explanation. "I'm not ready, Cooper. We were just standing here talking about Daniel."

"I know that. But Jude, Daniel is gone. I'm sorry. I know that sounds harsh. I miss him every damn day. I was sanding that table, thinking of when we were planning how to design it. I still keep expecting him to walk into the shop and tell me about some new job he and Logan are setting up. I drive past a property that comes up for sale, I still reach for my phone to call him.

"But he's not here. And if you and I both miss him, what if we missed him together?"

I closed my eyes, feeling the weight of the day closing in on me. "Cooper, when you kissed me, how was it? How did it feel?"

He raised one eyebrow. "Are you fishing, Jude? You're a great kisser. I've always thought you were attractive."

"But did you feel anything? Like. . .sparks? You know?"

Cooper looked around the room, up at the ceiling, anywhere but my eyes. Finally, he shook his head.

"Not sparks. But that could come. And my God, Jude, we're not kids. Maybe that's the kind of thing you only get when you're young."

"That's the most depressing thing I've ever heard. So now we're old and washed up?"

"No! Or—I don't know. Dammit, Jude, I'm trying to do a good thing here. You and me together makes sense, right?"

I took his hand again, squeezing it between both of mine. "Of course, it makes sense, sweetie. I love you, and I will always love you. But you're my friend. We can remember Daniel, and miss him together, without this." I pointed to his lips and then to my own. "And Cooper, I'm greedy. If I were ever to want. . .more someday, again, I want it all. I don't want to settle. I want sparks. I want—" I closed my eyes and smiled. "I want the magic, like when you're dancing with someone and you look up at him. . .and the world stands still." I shivered, as remembering, the feeling washed over me again.

Cooper heaved a sigh. "So. . .nothing? You felt nothing?"

I bit my lip and glanced up at him through my eyelashes. I shook my head.

Cooper pressed his lips together and nodded slowly. And then one side of his mouth quirked up.

"Daniel would die laughing at us right now." He chuckled, and I couldn't help joining him.

Before long, we were both crying with laughter, clutching our sides and leaning against the walls.

"I *kissed* you! Because I thought Daniel would want me to! God, what the hell was I thinking?" Cooper doubled over again.

"Spark! No spark!" I gasped, holding my middle.

Finally, when the laughter had subsided to wheezes, I patted Cooper's shoulder.

"I don't know what's got into you guys. First Matt takes me to dinner, and unless I'm imagining it, he almost put the moves on me. You here, tonight. And Logan—" I stopped and looked down.

"What about Logan?" I heard the curiosity in Cooper's tone.

I waved my hand. "Oh, nothing. You know Logan, he's just coming around a lot, keeping his eye on me. And then the other night. . ." I bit my lip. The dance and near-kiss was not something I was ready to share. For some reason, it felt more sacred than what had just happened with Cooper. I shook my head.

"The other night?" Cooper prompted.

"I'm being silly. I was going to say that if I didn't know better, I'd expect Eric to come by next, offer to bring me on as Janet's sister-wife." I winked at Cooper. "That might not be a bad gig."

Cooper rolled his eyes, and I laughed again.

"Okay, I got to get home." I smiled up at him. "Thanks for this. I needed it."

Cooper lifted a hand. "I'm glad I could help. Even if there's no spark, at least I can provide comic relief."

"Which is exactly what I wanted tonight. I'll talk to you next week, Cooper." I turned, but before I reached the door, I stopped and looked back him, still standing by the unfinished table.

"Cooper, that spark? Don't give up on it. Not yet. You're going to find someone who can give it to you."

Chapter Ten

Logan

EVER SINCE HIGH SCHOOL GRADUATION, the posse had made sure to get together at least once a month. At first it hadn't been difficult; even when Daniel and I went away to college, we were less than an hour away and regularly back in the Cove. The girlfriends, and then the wives, were included in most of our plans, but the ones who stuck, like Jude, Samantha and Janet, were wise enough to give us boys our time alone, too.

When I had designed my house, I had included a room that was especially for the posse. From the solid oak bar in the corner, with its built-in coolers and ice-maker, to the pool table and state-of-the-art sound system, it was a man's room. Over the years, I had added framed photos of the group and other mementos. It was, I thought, our unofficial clubhouse.

I sat on my leather barstool and watched as Matt chalked a cue. Eric and Cooper were playing, too, but it was one of their more laid-back games. No high stakes here tonight. It was a Friday night, and after a few beers, we were all feeling pretty mellow.

"So, Matt." Mark tossed a handful of nuts into his mouth and munched. "Remember when we talked about you guys dating my sister? What happened? How did you end up with her friend instead?"

We all knew the answer, but it was much more fun to rib Matt about it than to admit that. He ignored Mark for a few minutes as he lined up his shot and pocketed a few balls.

He straightened before leaning his cue against the table and picking up his beer. "I have no freaking clue. All I can tell you is I took Jude out to dinner one night. I didn't put the moves on her, because. . .well, hell. Because she's *Jude*. I thought I'd lay the groundwork, you know? Wine and dine her before I—"

Mark yelled, clapping his hands over his ears. "My sister! She's my sister. Keep it PG-13, please." He shuddered.

Matt shrugged. "You asked. Anyway, before I could ask her out again, she had that thing at that Tide, and then on the way—you know what happened. I met Sandra."

"But you weren't supposed to be picking up other girls. You were supposed to be courting my sister." Mark had moved on to pretzels, and he jabbed one in Matt's direction to make his point.

Matt grimaced and cracked his knuckles. "I don't know what to tell you, man. I love Jude. Like I love my sisters, you know? I tried to look at her different when we were at dinner that night, but I just kept thinking of her like Molly or Ellen. And then she brought up kids, and I started thinking. You know what? I want kids. I want to be a dad."

I sipped my bottle of beer. "Is Sandra on board with that?"

"We haven't gone far down that road, but yeah, I've been honest. She has Lily, and she's a great kid. But Sandra says she never planned to have an only child." He picked up his cue again and ran his fingers down the shaft. "It's early days yet. I'm not jumping into anything, not without being as sure as I can be. But we're a good fit so far." He looked up and met my eyes. "You guys like her, right?"

I smiled. "She's terrific. Fits in real well. I'm glad it worked out for you, buddy."

"So then there were two." Eric blew an easy shot and cursed without any heat. "Cooper and Logan. You want to give us a status report, too? Nosy minds want to know." He waggled his eyebrows at Cooper, and Mark groaned.

Cooper looked uncomfortable as he stepped around the table and eyed up his shot. He leaned over, squinting, and the room was silent as he flicked the ball.

Balls scattered, sliding into pockets with satisfying clicks. Cooper stretched his back and glanced at me.

"What do you want to know?" He stalked around the car and dug around in the cooler. "Shit, Logan, I'm done with beer for the night. Mind if I pull out the good stuff?"

I spread my hand in a help-yourself gesture. Cooper rummaged in the small fridge and emerged with a bottle of Jack. He pulled a shot glass from the shelf, filled it and downed it in one smooth move.

"What do you want to know?" he repeated, looking around. "What I did with Jude? You want the dirty details? Shut up, Mark." He glared as our friend opened his mouth. "We all get it. So plug your ears or take this chance to hit the head while I give the people what they want." He poured another shot and downed it just as fast.

"You all want to know how I seduced Jude."

My breath hissed in between clenched teeth, and my hands balled into fists. "Son of a bitch, that was never part of the—"

"What, Logan? Part of the plan? I don't remember us laying down guidelines. No one gave me a rulebook. It was just sweep Jude off her feet and may the best man win. Remember?" He grinned. "Well, maybe you're looking at the best man."

"You—" I jumped to my feet and would have sailed over the bar if Eric hadn't grabbed my arm.

"What?" Cooper repeated. "Why are you getting so sore? It's what we agreed on, right?"

"Cooper, I think you need to shut up for a minute." Matt's face was pinched as he approached the bar.

I stepped back, holding onto my cool with the thinnest of threads. Mark patted my shoulder and glanced between Cooper and me.

"Want to tell us what's going on? Cooper, did something really happen with you and Jude?"

"Why, don't you think I'm good enough for her?" Cooper raised one eyebrow.

"Of course not. None of you are good enough for my sister. But I'm pretty damn sure if something did happen, Jude would've told my wife, and my wife would've told me. So I'm wondering what you're playing at here."

Cooper held his gaze steady for a minute more before he sighed and rolled his shoulders. "Nothing. Nothing happened with Jude and me. Well, I kissed her," he amended. "But that's all, and it didn't go any further. And it won't."

"Why not?" They had abandoned all pretense of continuing the game, and Matt leaned against the table.

Cooper raised one shoulder. "No spark. That's what she said, anyway. And she was right. I mean, kissing her was fun. It was great. But it was, you know. . ." He searched for a word. "Comfortable. You know when you're kissing a girl, and you get to the point where if you have to stop, you feel like you're going to die?"

We all looked around the room, down at the floor, as we nodded.

Cooper sighed. "That didn't happen. If I had kept kissing her, if things had, you know, heated up, that would have been fine. But things didn't heat up, and that was fine, too."

"What did Jude think? What did she say?" Mark, feeling it was safe, moved away from me and took a seat. "She said there was no spark?"

"Yeah. And when I told her that was all right, the spark might come later, but I was okay with comfortable for now, she told me she wasn't. She said she wants the magic." Cooper turned his eyes to me. "She said something about dancing with someone. And I could be way off-base, totally wrong, but to me, it sounded like she was talking about something recent. I don't think she meant Daniel."

"So you think she's already seeing someone?" Eric's voice was incredulous.

"No." Cooper shook his head. "I think she would have told me. She joked about all of us taking her out, she mentioned

Matt and me, and she started to say something about Logan, but then she stopped."

"Logan?" Mark used his best no-nonsense classroom voice. "Do you have something to share with us?"

Slumping back on the stool, I shrugged. "No. I mean, I've been seeing her in the mornings, when she opens, but just to make sure she's okay. And I saw her the other night. I helped her at the Tide when she was cleaning the kitchen."

"You want to explain why you almost took off my head when I was kidding around before about seducing Jude?" Cooper kept his eyes level on my face. "You didn't exactly seem casual."

I held his gaze. "Nope. Just sounded like you weren't taking it seriously."

"It was more than that." Matt cocked his head. "You have something to say, Logan? Say it."

Cooper broke the stretching silence. "After Jude left the other night, I got to thinking about you, Logan. There was something in her voice when she mentioned your name. Different than when she talks about the rest of us."

Matt tossed his empty beer bottle into the barrel. It hit the others with a jarring rattle. "When I talked to you the night I took Jude to dinner, something was off with you. I got a vibe. What gives?"

It fell to Mark as the older brother to ask me the question. "Do you *like* Jude, Logan?"

That broke us, and the tension vanished. The laughter went beyond the humor of Mark's question and was tinged with relief. Spats within our group were rare, and uncomfortable for all of us. And we'd never yet fought over a woman.

Matt slapped a hand on my back. "Spill it, brother. No secrets here. Remember when you liked Karen Martin? Did we tell anyone?"

I snorted. "Matt, that was fifth grade."

"Right, and we never said anything in all these years. We're trustworthy."

I shook my head. "Cooper, pour me a shot, would you? If I'm going to spill my guts, I need some Jack."

"Shots all around, Coop," suggested Eric.

We downed them without speaking. I closed his eyes, savoring the burn. I could feel all eyes on me as he spoke.

"Okay. Yes. I *like* Jude."

"When did this happen?" There was no condemnation in Mark's voice.

"I don't know. It wasn't like I just woke up one day feeling that way." I heaved out a breath. In for a penny, in for a pound, I decided.

"I always kind of liked Jude. But I never would do anything to get between her and Daniel. They were—well, you guys saw it. They were Jude and Daniel."

They nodded. Everyone knew exactly what I meant.

"And it's not like I hung around waiting for something to happen. You know how I felt about Daniel."

Eric punched my arm. "Never any doubt, bro. We all know that."

"But why didn't you say something when we made this agreement?" Matt wasn't condemning, just confused. "If you had told us, Cooper and I could have saved ourselves a lot of trouble. I mean, I asked Karl for dating advice. Karl, who works for me? I sank that low."

"Yeah, man, and I kissed her," Cooper put in.

I pinned him with a glare. "Don't remind me. I still kind of want to hit you."

Cooper put up his hands. "No spark, remember? I'm not your competition, dude. And if you'd told us up front, I never would have kissed her."

"I didn't want to sound—you know, we'd just spread Daniel's ashes. Saying I thought I was in love with his widow seemed a little like jumping the gun."

"You're in love with her?" Eric's mouth dropped.

I put my head into my hands, leaning on the bar. "I don't know. I think so. And sometimes I think maybe she might—" I shook my head. "I don't want to scare her off. I don't want to lose her friendship."

Cooper slung an arm around my shoulder. "I have a feeling that's not going to be a problem. She had a look on her face. And there was her voice, too. You might have to man up and go for it."

There were more nods around the room before Matt shot to his feet.

"What the hell's the matter with us? Sitting around here talking about feelings and love and shit? When did we become a bunch of old ladies?"

Grunts of approval followed his proclamation.

"Another round of shots!" Cooper slapped his hand on the bar. "And then. . .we shoot pool. Crank up that music, Mark. The men are back."

Chapter Eleven

Jude

"**C**OOPER *KISSED YOU?*" SAMANTHA NEARLY shrieked the words, and they echoed through the empty restaurant. It was slow, even for a cloudy off-season Wednesday, and against their strong objections, I had sent Sadie and Mack home a few hours early. I didn't often get the chance to talk to my sister-in-law in person without kids, men and customers milling around.

"You want to say that a little louder, Sam? I don't think Meggie caught it up in Savannah."

Samantha clapped her hand over her mouth. "Sorry. But oh my God, Jude. *Cooper?* What did you do?"

I shrugged. "At first, I kissed him back. I thought, why not?"

"But then. . .?" Samantha leaned forward. Her curly brown hair fell over one shoulder, and she flicked it back impatiently.

"But then, there was nothing. All I could think about was what I was going to say after he stopped. And how his hand was pushing my bra hook into my spine. I'm sorry, if you're lost in a kiss, you're not thinking about that stuff."

"Not if it's a good kiss."

"Right. So I stopped him, and we talked a little. And then we laughed. A lot. Until we cried."

Sam shook her head. "That's crazy. What was he thinking?"

I wiped off the counter and dropped my rag into the sink. "I guess that we were both single, so maybe we should be single together." I frowned and shook my head. "Or not. I don't know. I'm not sure Cooper really knew why he did it. But it's over, no hard feelings."

"The only one who hasn't made his move yet is Logan." Sam played with the wrapper of her straw and glanced up slyly. She raised one eyebrow when my cheeks went hot.

"Or did he? C'mon, Jude, you're blushing. What are you not telling me?"

"Geez, Sam, are we in high school again? Calm down."

Samantha rolled her eyes. "When you live in small town, you never really leave high school. And I'm living vicariously through you. I love your brother, don't get me wrong. He's my one and only. But you gotta admit Logan is hot. Always has been. I couldn't understand why he never got married."

I bit my lip. "Remember Tess? I think when she died, he just shut down that part of his life. It was so sad."

"I'd forgotten about her. Mark and I were still living up in Jacksonville then. It was over twenty years ago. They were engaged, right?"

I nodded. "Yes. She died three months before the wedding. It was sudden, a bacterial infection. She was fine, then she was really sick, and then she was gone. It all happened in about a week."

"That's horrible." Sam was silent for a beat. "But from the red in your cheeks, I'm guessing Logan is ready to move on. What happened?"

"Nothing, really. I'm probably making more out of it than it means."

"I'll be the judge of that. Tell me all."

"I was here by myself, and you know I like to dance while I'm cleaning. Logan came in, and he danced with me. And then the music got slow, and he danced with me some more, but slower. . .and I thought he was going to kiss me. Just for min-ute, he looked at me. . . but then he pulled back." I lifted one shoulder. "And that was it."

"But do you think he's—" A beeping sound interrupted Samantha, and she glanced at her phone. "Shit! I have a meet-ing at Gavin's school. They're trying to rope me into being class mom again. I'm going to stand my ground this year and say no."

I grinned. "You say that every time. And this is Gavin's last year in elementary school. You know you're going to do it."

Sam sighed and climbed down from the stool. "Yeah, I am. You were the smart one, you know, having your kids young. I don't know what I was thinking when Mark and I decided to wait. And then to have four! I'm too old for this."

She circled the bar to hug me before grabbing her handbag and heading for the door.

"We'll talk again soon. I need to hear more about your hot love life!"

I shook my head, smiling. Growing up with only a brother,

91

I hadn't realized how much I missed having a sister until I had one in Samantha. Now I didn't know what I would do without this crazy lady who had become my best friend.

I began gathering all the towels and rags, tossing them into a basket. Doing a load of laundry now would save me time after closing. If things didn't pick up soon, I was going to close early and go home for a nap, I decided.

"Mom."

Bent over to pick up a pile of towels, I hadn't heard the door open, and I jerked upright. Joseph was standing just on the other side of the bar, looking for me.

"Joseph!" I dropped the basket and rounded the bar. "What are you doing here? Are you okay? Why didn't you tell me you were coming down?"

I hugged my son, who towered over me by a full head, and then pulled back to look at his face. What I saw there took my breath away.

Joseph's eyes were red and bleak. His mouth was tight, and his jaw clenched. I was reminded of the days immediately after Daniel had died, when I would come upon my son holed up by himself, not wanting his sister or me to see him cry.

"Baby, what's wrong?" I began to pull him toward a table and then stopped. "Meggie? Is Meggie okay?"

Joseph nodded and spoke for the first time since he'd said my name. "I guess so. I mean, I haven't talked to her in a while, but she texted me yesterday."

I blew out a sigh. Something was tearing him up, but as long as both of my babies were alive and whole, I could handle anything.

"Sit down." I pointed to the chair and sat across from him. "Do you want something to drink? Are you hungry?"

"No, thanks. Mom, I need to talk to you." His lip almost quivered, but he clamped down again and scowled. "It's important."

"Okay. So talk." When he opened his mouth and closed it again, I reached across the table to cover his hand. "It's all right, baby. Nothing is so bad we can't fix it, between us." I swallowed. "You're not sick, are you?"

He shook his head. "No, Mom. I'm sorry, I didn't mean to scare you like that. I didn't even think that you would assume—no. I'm okay." He gripped my hand and took a deep breath.

"Remember Lindsay, Mom?"

I frowned. "The girl you were dating last year? Yes, of course. Pretty, smart—she was going to school to be a vet, right?"

Joseph nodded. "Yeah, she was." He set his jaw again, and I thought I could hear his teeth grinding.

"Last year, remember when I went back to school? We thought Dad was going to be okay for a little while longer, and he told me to go back. He said I should."

"Yes, I remember." That whole time was a blur. Joseph had announced midway through the summer that he was taking a break from school so he could help me with Daniel, who had been declining quickly. When he seemed to rally for a few weeks, he'd insisted that his son should return to college, saying that I would need him more later. Three weeks after Joseph went back, I had had to call him home. He and Meggie had just made it to the house before Daniel passed.

"I was so messed up, Mom. I was scared about Dad, and I

was partying too much." Tears began to run down his face, and he no longer tried to hide them.

"One night, I got really drunk. Lindsay got me home, and I just lost it. I was crying, and she was, you know, holding me. Trying to make me feel better."

I felt dread rising within my heart. "Okay."

Joseph choked on a sob. "We slept together, Mom. And I wasn't smart. We didn't—I didn't take precautions, like you and Dad always said. I was stupid and drunk."

"Okay." It was all I could get out. I held onto the word like a raft in the storm.

"So then I came home, when you called me, and then Dad. . ." His whole body shook. "Then Dad was gone." He laid his head on the table. I moved my hand to stroke his head.

"What happened, Joseph? To Lindsay?"

He sniffed, hard, and raised his head, not quite meeting her eyes. "I emailed her. I told her I wasn't coming back to school, not then, and I didn't know when. And then I told her I needed a break, because I needed to be here for you and Meggie."

He took in a long breath. "I didn't hear anything back from her. I tried to email her a few times, I texted her, but she didn't answer. I figured she was pissed, and I was mad because I thought she could be more understanding. I mean, my dad had just died."

I nodded slowly. "Okay. And?"

"When I got back to school, I looked for her, and I asked around. Someone told me she had transferred to a school closer to home. She's from Clearwater, remember? So I sent her another email, just saying I was back at school, that I missed her. And then yesterday, she called me."

Joseph pulled his hands back and gripped the edge of the table. "She was pregnant, Mom. Lindsay had a baby. And it's mine."

The world spun just slightly, and I lost my breath for a moment. I mirrored Joseph's stance, holding the table as though it could keep me from sinking and drowning.

"Joseph. . ." I said his name on a breath, a long whisper.

"I'm sorry, Mom. I screwed up, I know. I'm so sorry. I-I just—" He cried a little more before he could speak again. "Having to come home and tell you is the hardest thing I've ever done."

I shook my head. "I don't think so, Joseph. This is life-changing. I think you're going to have lots of harder things coming right now." I ran a shaking hand through my hair, trying to make sense of life.

"It's a boy, Mom. The baby is a boy. I have a son."

In spite of myself, in contradiction to the tears running down my cheeks, I found a smile.

"Lindsay sent me a picture. We talked last night for a long, long time."

"Why didn't she tell you she was pregnant earlier? Joseph, forgive me, but I have to ask this—are you sure the baby is yours?"

He nodded. "Yeah. I'm sure. Lindsay is from a really conservative family. She had never—before me, I mean." He flushed. "And he looks like me. Look, Mom."

He pulled his phone from his back pocket and showed me

the screen. The startled face of an infant looked back at me, and after a moment of shock, I had to agree with Joseph. He looked just like my son had as a baby.

"She named him Daniel Joseph, and they call him DJ. When she told me that. . .Mom, I cried. I know I messed up, big time. I know I'm not ready to be a father. But I am, and I want to do a good job, like Dad. I want to make him proud."

"What are you going to do?" My head was spinning, and I couldn't imagine what Joseph must be feeling. Or Lindsay, the poor girl. . .going through a pregnancy and birth without the father of her baby.

"I'm driving down to Clearwater tonight." For the first time since he'd come into the restaurant, Joseph's voice was sure. "Lindsay didn't tell me about being pregnant because she didn't want to—after Dad—she said she wasn't sure I could handle it. But her family was great, and her parents have been helping her.

"I told her I wanted to see the baby and talk to her, so I'm going down there. I wanted to come and tell you in person, but I'm leaving right now. I want to get there before it gets too late."

I bit back a sarcastic remark about it already being too late. Bitterness wasn't going to change anything now.

"Mom." Joseph held my hand again. "Do you hate me? Are you disappointed?"

I drew in a deep breath. "Joseph, of course, I don't hate you. I could never hate you. And no, I'm not even disappointed in you. I'm disappointed *for* you. This is going to change how you live your life." I thought of the plans and dreams Daniel and I had had for our son. "But you know, it doesn't need to mean the end of your life, or of Lindsay's. I'll do whatever I can to help you. It's going to be hard work for you both, I'm not going to sugar-coat it. But this doesn't change how I feel about you. Nothing ever could."

Tears swimming in his eyes again, Joseph wrapped me in tight hug. "I love you, Mom. Thank you."

I patted his back, determined not to break down until he left. "I love you, too, baby. Now you better get on the road. Please be careful. Text me when you get there."

He kissed my cheek and was out the door. I watched him drive out of sight and then collapsed into my chair.

I laid my head on the table and cried.

Chapter Twelve

Logan

I PULLED INTO THE PARKING LOT of the Rip Tide about half an hour after Joseph had left. I saw Jude's car in its usual spot and the closed sign on the door.

I half-expected the door to be locked—maybe I hoped it would be—but the knob turned easily in my hand. I bit back a sigh at her tendency to ignore locks and went into the restaurant.

Jude sat at the bar. The lights were dim, but I could see that she was rolling a shot glass across the dark wood.

"Jude."

She jumped a mile and for a moment I was afraid she would fall off the barstool. But once she spied me, she righted herself.

"Logan. Come in. Or, come over. I see you've already come in."

Someone who didn't know Jude, who hadn't known her for thirty years, might have mistaken the precision of her words for sobriety. I, however, knew better.

"What're we drinking, Jude?" Turning the lock on the outside door, I made my way to where she sat.

Jude grinned up at me. Her eyes were lined in red, and my heart broke a little more for her.

"I'm drinking Uncle John's limoncello, Logan. This is an occasion, after all. Time to break out the good stuff.

I spied the bottle of sunny yellow liquor sitting on the bar next to Jude. Her uncle John lived in New Jersey and bottled his own lemon liqueur. He sent down bottles each holiday, and I remembered it was Jude's favorite indulgence, whether she was celebrating or drowning sorrows.

She walked carefully around the bar and pulled out another shot glass. Placing it next to hers, she uncapped the bottle and tipped it over.

"How many of those have you had, Jude?"

She finished pouring, set the bottle upright and replaced the top. "I lost count after five. But now you're here to help me count."

She propped her elbows on the bar, picked up her glass and raised it to eye level. "To. . .life. Screwed up as it is."

I followed suit, lifting my drink. "To life."

Jude slammed hers down, closing her eyes and breathing out.

I drank my own, my eyes never leaving Jude. She still sat with her elbows up, thrusting her breasts into prominence. She'd taken down her hair at some point, and it was tousled around her shoulders. Even knowing what she was going through, I found it hard to breathe, watching her.

She opened her eyes and stared up into mine. For a long moment, she didn't speak, and then she licked her lips.

"Don't you want to know what we're celebrating, Logan?"

I couldn't resist. I reached out and hooked one strand of hair on my finger. "I think I have a pretty good idea."

"Really? I'd bet against you on that." She poured another drink.

"Jude, maybe you've had enough." But I drank what she poured me.

"Not nearly. So how would you know why I broke out the limoncello, Logan? Is that part of your mission in life? To keep your eye on me? Make sure I don't go off the deep end?" She smiled, wide and almost sleepy, and I felt his heart skip.

"I know because Joseph called me on the way out of town. He was worried about you. He told me the whole story, asked me to come over and make sure you were okay."

"Okay." Jude dropped her head to the bar and laughed. "Yeah, I'm okay. What a stupid. . ." Her voice trailed off.

I smoothed her hair, let my hand rest in the crook of her neck. "I know. That was a dumb thing to say. Okay must be the last thing you're feeling."

Jude raised her head just enough to look at me. "Logan. . .I'm a *grandmother*. Did he tell you that? He has a baby. He got a girl pregnant." She put her head down again.

"Jude, I know this has to be. . .devastating." I wasn't sure that was the right word, but it would do for now. "But it isn't the end of the world. Joseph is a good kid. He made a mistake, sure, but that doesn't mean—"

"I know." She turned her head so that her cheek lay on the

bar. "He's a good kid. Daniel and I. . .we used to say, we've got good kids. Sure, they have their ups and downs. All of them do. And I never thought they were perfect. But I did think I'd always have Daniel there to go through it with me, when they had their downs. But I don't. Today when Joseph came to tell me, I kept thinking. . .why am I doing this alone? Where is Daniel when I need him?"

I closed my eyes and moved my hand around to caress her cheek. "But you're not alone, Jude. You never have to be."

She didn't respond, and this time I was the one to pour another round. I needed that last shot of courage.

With the burn still on my tongue, I leaned over the bar. Jude's eyes were heavy but not shut. She glanced at me sideways.

"What are you doing, Logan?" The words were whispered, just a breath that feathered my mouth.

"I don't know." I whispered, too, as though there were anyone to hear us. "But I think I'm going to kiss you."

I lowered my mouth, bringing my lips softly on Jude's. The moment we touched, something surged through me, straight to my groin. I groaned and leaned farther over, so that my mouth took full possession of Jude's, no longer a simple kiss but full involvement of our lips and tongues.

I had expected a protest, or at best, a sleepy acquiescence. Instead, she answered my moan and opened her mouth, aggressively meeting stroke with stroke. Without lifting her head, she angled so that she had better access, and one hand came up to clutch at my hair.

I moved my hand down her back, as far as I could reach, but I wanted more. I stroked down her cheek, running my fingers over the smoothness of her skin to her neck. I paused to feel the tripping pulse just above her collarbone, and then traced the bone before lowering my touch to the rise of her breasts. She gasped, both then and again when I slid a finger beneath the fabric of her tank top, beneath the bra, just barely grazing a nipple.

My heart pounding, my head spinning from both the effects of the limoncello and her closeness, I pulled away from her mouth just long enough to grip her gently beneath the arms.

"Logan—"

"Shh." I lifted her carefully up onto the bar, swinging her around and stepping back so that I stood between her legs. With better access now, I pulled her head down toward my own and plundered her mouth. Jude wrapped her arms around my neck, burying her hands in my hair.

I dragged my lips down her neck, my mouth now following the trail my hands had made. I pushed aside the thin cotton of her shirt and used one finger to slide the strap of her bra aside. I covered one breast with my mouth, laving the nipple through her bra. Jude moaned and held my head in place, her fingers gripping my skull.

I pulled the cup of her bra aside and suckled, while my hand rolled the other nipple. Desire rose higher in me, throbbing between my legs, and while my mouth moved to the other breast, my hand stroked down her stomach to the snap of her shorts. I pulled it apart, but the angle was awkward. Instead, holding her around the back with one arm, I brought the other hand to the leg of her shorts and brushed within, just touching the cotton of her underwear.

"Logan." It was a groan, as she leaned back to give me more access. I touched her first over the dampness of the material and then slipped two fingers within. Jude arched her neck back on a hiss of breath.

I kissed up the column of her throat to her ear lobe. "Jude, my God, you're beautiful."

She dropped her head onto my shoulder. "Do you want to go upstairs? To the apartment?"

I couldn't believe she was asking me the question. The answer, of course, was yes. When it came to Jude, my answer had always been yes. It always would be yes.

I turned her sideways and threaded an arm beneath her knees, scooping her up and holding her against my chest. Lowering my head, I caught her lips again, and moved carefully around the tables and chairs until we reached the steps. I climbed one step at a time, keeping Jude's head away from the wall.

It had been years since I'd been in the small apartment, but even in the semi-darkness, I could see the open bedroom door. I pushed the door wider with my foot and lay Jude on the bed.

The buzz from limoncello had given way to the high of touching Jude, kissing her. I leaned on one knee, the mattress dipping as I balanced with one hand on either side of her head. I kissed her once softly before I gripped the hem of her tee and pulled it over her head. Tossing it to the side, I unbuttoned and shrugged off my own dress shirt and lay down, reveling in the feel of her skin against mine.

Jude ran her hands down my back, kissing my shoulders and then turning my head back toward her so that she could cover my lips. Her nails on my arms raised goosebumps. I slid a hand beneath her and unhooked her bra, catching my breath as I palmed her breast. My lips skimmed over her chest, and I sucked at one nipple, even as my hand covered the other.

Jude's breath hitched. She trailed her hands to the top of my pants and fumbled with the button.

"Hold on," I murmured. I eased her shorts down, kissing down her legs and unhitching them when they caught on her feet. I stood up for just a minute to shuck off his pants, and then returned my mouth to Jude's stomach, dragging lower and lower until I met the top of her cotton panties.

There was so much I wanted to do, so many things I wanted to experience with Jude, but the pulsing desire made me impatient. I hooked my fingers beneath her underwear, tugging down. Jude mirrored my actions with my boxers, and in moments, nothing was between us.

I slipped my fingers low, parting her legs and dragging one fingertip over her folds, groaning again when she arched her back as though desperate to get closer to my hand. I eased a single finger within her as I used my thumb to massage the small knob of nerves. She writhed, breathing hard.

"Logan, my God. Please. . ." Her voice was filled with raw passion, and I knew I could not wait a minute longer. I held myself over her, lacing my fingers with hers and holding her gaze before I plunged inside her.

I was still for a moment, and then we both began to move. My eyes stayed steady on Jude as I lifted myself up, pulling nearly all way out, and then thrusting hard into her again. I wanted to savor this, to hold onto every second so I'd never forget how it felt to be inside her. I'd waited my entire life to be this close to the woman I loved, and I didn't want to rush it.

But I could feel the building momentum within Jude and my own body, too. She was making sexy little gasps of need, her fingernails digging into my back as she urged me closer and faster. I fought to keep control until Jude jerked her hips upwards and cried out. Then I was gone. I gasped as she tightened around me, and I called her name as I emptied myself deep within her.

When I could think again, I held myself on my elbows and knees, keeping my weight from Jude. Her eyes had drifted shut, and I brushed kisses over each lid. Her lips curved into a smile.

Easing away slightly, I lay down next to her. She turned, eyes still closed, and cuddled into me. I fumbled with a blanket folded at the end of the bed, pulling it over us.

"Logan, don't leave me, 'kay?" Her words were so soft, I almost didn't hear them.

With a tenderness that was only the tip of my love for this woman, I brushed a lock of hair from her forehead, pressing a kiss onto her heated skin.

"Never."

Chapter Thirteen

Jude

OPENED MY EYES TO BRIGHT sunshine. Groaning, I covered my face and rolled over, stopping abruptly when I ran into the hard body in bed with me.

Logan.

I sat up too fast and felt the morning-after effects of the limoncello. Dropping my head into my hands, I tried to sit very still, just until the room stopped spinning.

"Morning."

Memories from the night before washed over me, and I was positive that my blush reached places I didn't even want to consider. Logan's hand brushed over my bare back and skimmed lower. I groaned.

I wasn't sure, but I thought I heard him chuckle. If it hadn't required moving, I might have reached over to smack him.

"Your head hurt?"

I peeked out from one hand. "What do you think?" My

voice was thick, and my mouth felt as though like I'd eaten a bag of cotton balls.

"I think you need coffee, maybe with a little something in it."

I gasped and jumped out of bed, my heart pounding. "The sun! My God, what time is it? The Tide, I'm late! People are going to be waiting. . ." I trailed off, abruptly aware that I was completely naked and that Logan was enjoying the view.

I yanked the blanket off the bed and wrapped it around me. "Would you please stop? You're staring at me."

"Yes, I am." He leaned toward me, as though to snag the blanket, and I skirted out of reach.

"Logan, did you hear me? I'm—" I squinted at the old digital clock next to the bed. "Shit, it's almost eight. I'm two hours late opening the Tide."

He sat up, and the sheet sagged dangerously low around his waist. My eyes ranged over his chest, the defined pecs and abs and the trail of light brown hair that trailed down—

I closed my eyes as the room swung around again. *My God, I slept with Logan.*

He was speaking, and I tried to focus on his words, not on his chest.

"Yes, it's almost eight. And yes, the Tide is going to open late today. But guess what, sugar? The world isn't ending. Calm down."

I perched on the edge of the bed, still clutching the blanket. "People are going to know. Your car is parked in the lot, right? And when my regulars showed up at six, expecting their breakfast, they saw *my* car, and they saw *your* car. And a locked door."

"Is that such a bad thing?" Logan found his boxers, stood and pulled them on. I averted my gaze as memories of the night before burned. I couldn't think of that now. It was all too much, too confusing on top of the mess that was my life. I dropped back onto the bed, throwing an arm over my eyes. On second thought, maybe hiding up here wasn't a bad option.

I felt Logan's finger trace my cheekbones. "Jude, take a breath. Get a shower. I'll go down and start the coffee, turn on the grills. If anyone asks, I'll explain you weren't feeling well last night, slept here and called me to come over to help this morning. Okay?"

I nodded, not quite ready to trust my voice yet. I sensed Logan moving around the room, pulling on clothes. I heard him go into the bathroom, and when he passed me a few minutes later, heading for the steps, I reached out to catch his hand.

"Logan, thank you." I swallowed. "For this. And for last night."

He was still for a moment, then his hand turned within mine and squeezed it. "Jude, I hope by now you know I'd do anything for you."

I didn't answer, and he kissed my hand before releasing it.

I listened to his footsteps on the stairs. I didn't move until the scent of coffee drifted up to me, at which point I dragged my sore body to the bathroom.

The shower helped. I stood beneath the stream as bits and pieces of the night before flashed in my mind.

Joseph. I cursed out loud, remembering that I had told him to text me when he'd arrived safely in Clearwater. Of course, about the time he would have been texting, I had been. . .busy. Heat that had nothing to do with the water temperature sluiced down my center.

I shut off the water and toweled myself dry, glad that I always kept a few extra pairs of shorts, T-shirts and a change of underwear in the apartment. I dressed quickly and had just stepped into the sitting room when Logan climbed the steps, holding a steaming mug of coffee.

"I need to find my phone." I blurted the words without thinking and wanted to kick myself.

When a man brings you coffee, say thank you.

One side of Logan's mouth lifted, and he pulled my phone from his back pocket. I took it from his hand and then accepted the mug, sipping and sighing in appreciation as the sweetness tinged with something else slid down my throat.

"I put a little Bailey's in. Not much, just enough to get you over the hump this morning." Logan grinned and tucked a strand of hair behind my ear. "And Joseph made it safely to Clearwater about seven-thirty last night."

I quirked a brow at him over the rim of my mug. "Did you look at my messages?"

"No." He rolled his eyes. "He texted me, too. To check on you."

"Oh." I took another drink of coffee. "Was there anyone downstairs?"

"No. Sadie and Mack just got here, so I turned everything over to them. I told them you'd had a rough night."

"Yeah, you could say that again." I set my coffee on the table and pulled out a chair. "Logan, I want to thank you again for last night."

He sat down across from me, legs spread wide and a hand on each knee. "I think maybe I should be thanking you."

My cheeks burned. "That's not what I meant. I was talking about you coming over so I didn't have to be alone." I toyed with the edge of my shorts. "I don't know what I would have done if you hadn't come. Probably passed out in the bar. Sadie would've had a heart attack when she came in this morning and found me."

"Jude." I looked up, hearing the serious tone in his voice. "I know you got hit with a lot last night. What happened between us—I didn't mean to make your life more complicated. But it wasn't because I was trying to make you feel better. It wasn't because I'd been drinking. What we did last night, I've been wanting to do for a very long time."

My mouth sagged a little. "You did? Wait. Just. . .Logan, what are you talking about?"

He reached across the table and covered my hand. "I'd rather not get into that right now, when you're still slightly hung over, worried about Joseph and itching to get downstairs. I was thinking maybe we could have dinner tonight." He licked his lips, and I realized he was nervous.

"Tonight?" My mind darted about madly.

"Yes." Logan nodded. "You know. A date. The thing most people do before they do what we did last night."

I swallowed. "Okay, but what if Joseph needs me? What if he comes back tonight?"

Logan sighed. "Jude, do you really think he's going to drive back here today, after he just got to Clearwater last night to meet the son he didn't know he had?"

I ran a hand over my hair, lifting it off my neck and wishing I had a ponytail holder. It was warm in the apartment, which didn't help with my already-shot nerves.

"No, you're probably right." I met Logan's eyes, and my heart sped up when I saw his expression. It was soft and understanding, mixed with something else I wasn't ready to name.

"Tell you what." He stood, stretching. "I need to get home, get changed. Go into the office for a little while. I'll call you right after lunch. By then, you should have heard from Joseph. If he tells you he's coming home, we'll put off our date for a few days. But if not, I'll pick you up at your house at seven. Sound like a deal?"

I found myself nodding before I could really think about it. Logan smiled and leaned over me, trapping me in the chair with his arms on either side.

"Meanwhile, think about this today." He kissed me, and it wasn't the sort of see-you-later peck I might have expected. His lips coaxed mine open, and his tongue moved within my mouth until I responded in kind. Almost against my will, I lifted my arms to wrap around his neck and arched closer, barely even noticing the low moan that escaped me.

Logan finally broke away, softening the separation by

trailing his lips down my neck and then returning for one final soft touch at my mouth.

"I'll see you tonight." He straightened and touched my cheek before leaving.

I sat perfectly still after he left, one hand covering my mouth. In the space of less than twenty-four hours, my world had been turned upside down—again. And I wasn't entirely sure what to make of it.

With effort, I rose and headed downstairs to face Sadie and Mack.

Chapter Fourteen

SADIE AND MACK WERE ABNORMALLY quiet when I appeared in the restaurant. Sadie offered to fix me some eggs, and Mack poured me a new cup of coffee, adding just the right amount of cream. They sat me down on the deck, and Sadie fussed at me to eat while Mack covered the kitchen.

I had choked down about half of my eggs, with Sadie watching every move of my fork, when I finally lost it.

"Okay, what did Logan tell you?" I laid down my silverware and pinned Sadie with a glare. "You may as well spill it."

Sadie pursed her lips and looked away, toward the ocean. "I don't know what you mean."

"You're treating me the same way you did right after Daniel died, like I'm about to break. I want to know why."

"Well, there's no need to get testy, miss. Mind your tone." She softened the words by leaning over and patting my hand. "Logan told us about Joseph. He didn't want to, but Mack and I were so worried. We thought—when he said you hadn't felt well and had called him, why, we were thinking the worst. That there was something wrong with you." Sadie's soft blue eyes filled with tears.

"Oh." I looked down at my plate and drew in a breath. "I see."

"He wasn't talking behind your back," Sadie hurried to assure me. "He told us to ask you about it. But I think he knew you'd end up telling us yourself anyway."

I blinked back my own tears. I wasn't going to start the day off by crying, not again. "Sadie, I don't know what to do. Joseph isn't ready to be a father. He's just a boy still."

Sadie squeezed my hand. "None of them are, honey. They're all children until that baby comes along. Joseph's going to have to get up to speed faster than most, sure, but I know that boy. He's got a good head on his shoulders, and he's going to do what's right. You wait and see. Right now, it feels like the end of the world, but before long, you're going to look back on this as one of the biggest blessings in your life."

I sniffed and wiped at my eyes with a napkin. "You think so?"

"I know so." Sadie laughed. "A grandbaby! Just think! Maybe he didn't come along right when you would've liked him, but just you wait, you're going to love him to bits. And spoiled! I can't wait to get my hands on that baby. It's been a long time since any of mine were that little."

"Did Logan tell you the baby's name?" I picked up my fork, managed another bite of breakfast.

"No, what is it?" Sadie smiled expectantly.

"Daniel Joseph. She—Lindsay, that's the baby's mother— she calls him D.J." I drew in a long, shuddering breath. "That made me think she must be a decent girl, right? To name her baby after a man she didn't really know?"

Sadie sniffed and nodded. "Of course, she is. Joseph dated her, and maybe things aren't going in the exact order you wanted, but that's okay." She stood up and peered through the window into the kitchen. "Now I got to get back in there before that dang man of mine burns the pancakes. You finish eating, and then I'll put you to work."

Work was a balm, and I kept busy all morning. No one outside of Sadie and Mack seemed to have noticed my absence at opening time, though I knew I'd get some ribbing the next day when my early birds showed up.

Right before noon, my phone rang. When I saw Joseph's name, I stepped outside to answer the call.

"Mom? You okay?" The anxiety in my son's voice tugged at my heart, and my smiled.

"Yeah, baby. I'm fine. How are you, though? How is everything there?"

"Mom, it's amazing. The baby is so beautiful, and he's so smart! He lifts his head up, and he follows me around with his eyes. I think he knows I'm his dad. I know that's crazy, but I think he does."

I heard love and pride in every word, and my heart swelled. "Honey, I'm glad. I can't wait to see him, too. But how about Lindsay? How does she feel?"

He sighed. "She's amazing, too, Mom. I know you met her before, but I want you to really get to know her. Her parents were a little stiff at first. Her dad talked to me last night about responsibilities, and how I need to face up to mine. But he wasn't bad about it. He was kind of like Dad, you know?"

I felt tears on my cheeks and didn't even try to wipe them away. "Yes, I know what you mean. Joseph, I'm glad. I don't know if I could be so understanding if it were Meggie in the same situation. They sound like wonderful people."

"They really are." He was quiet for a minute. "I know I'm missing school, but I'm going to stay down here for a little while. I can't leave them right away. We have so much we need to work out."

I bit my lip. "I understand. Just keep me posted, okay?"

"I will. Oh, and tell Uncle Logan thanks again for me, will you? I hope you didn't mind that I called him and told him everything. I just thought you needed someone, and he seemed like the best person. I kind of thought he'd understand."

I kept my voice normal. "I'll tell him. Of course, I didn't mind. It was good to have Uncle Logan here to talk with me. I'm glad you called him."

After we hung up, with Joseph's promise to call every day still ringing in my ears, I leaned against the brick of the building and stared out at the ocean.

Had I told Joseph the truth? Was I glad he had called Logan, that Logan had come over and drunk limoncello with me? Definitely. Was I happy about what had happened next?

I just wasn't sure.

On one hand, if someone had asked me yesterday whether I wanted to date or was ready to move on with my life, I would have said no. Given the choice, I might never have moved on from Daniel.

But maybe it was like what Sadie had said. Just as fatherhood had been thrust on Joseph before he was quite ready, perhaps whatever this was with Logan was something I would never have sought, but needed.

Even with as much limoncello as I had consumed, I remembered every nuance of making love with Logan. Every touch, every moan, every movement of his lips. . .even now, with the damp sea air blowing around me, I could feel his touch.

It hadn't been awkward or uncomfortable. There hadn't even been a moment of uncertainty. On some level, it was as though I was meant to be with Logan, and my body had responded, even if my mind was a little slow to catch up.

I sighed and pushed off the building. Seven hours until I'd see him again, and I couldn't decide if I was dreading the evening. . .or dying of anticipation.

Chapter Fifteen

Jude

HAVING SEX FOR THE FIRST time in over eighteen months when I was mostly drunk was one thing. Having hours to think about it doing it again was quite another.

First I had to convince Sadie and Mack that it was safe to leave me. Sadie invited me home, offered to make dinner, repeatedly reminding me that I didn't have to be alone. I almost told them that I was going to spend the evening with Logan, but something held my tongue. I wasn't quite ready to go public with whatever was between us yet.

They stayed with me until five o'clock and walked me to the car. I waved, pasting what I hoped was a reassuring smile on my face. I drove home without seeing any of the familiar landmarks and pulled into the garage on autopilot.

I walked into the house that been my haven for nearly twenty years and tried to see it through Logan's eyes. Would he feel too much of Daniel's presence here? Would it make him uncomfortable? Last night, the apartment had been almost neutral territory. What if it were different tonight?

My phone buzzed, a text message from Meghan, just checking in. I dropped into a kitchen chair. I had promised Joseph I would tell Meggie about the baby, and getting it out of the way now seemed like a good idea.

That conversation lasted nearly forty-five minutes. Meghan was shocked; she cried, she railed against what she termed her brother's 'stupidity and irresponsibility'. But in the end, she decided she was more interested in her new nephew than in killing Joseph. She assured me that she would call him and wouldn't yell.

I wilted on my chair, exhausted again. After the day I had had, was it really wise to see Logan tonight? The only thing that kept me from canceling was the conviction that he just wouldn't take no for an answer.

I showered again, taking her time. I pulled out a new razor and paid special attention to parts of my body I hadn't worried about in many months. I washed my hair twice, conditioned it and rinsed until the water ran clear.

Wrapped in an oversized towel, I stood in front of the full-length mirror in my bedroom. Janet had given me a luscious new body cream for my birthday, and I rubbed it over her legs and arms with meticulous care. I dropped the towel to finish with my stomach and stopped, staring at my reflection.

Once upon a time, I remembered, I'd had a firm, taut middle, adequate breasts and smooth, supple skin. Everything had been where it was supposed to be before two children and twenty-five years of gravity. I'd always thought I had aged fairly well;

Daniel hadn't ever complained, and I'd been conscientious about exercise and eating smart.

But examining myself now, I saw bones jutting in my hips, a softly rounded stomach, breasts that had been through two pregnancies and a few years of nursing. It hadn't mattered so much to Daniel, because he had been with me at each stage. It had been his babies who changed my body. I wondered how Logan would look at me. Why would he want me when he could easily choose a younger woman with all her body parts in the right place?

The same doubt gnawed at me as I dressed, choosing a light and floaty cotton dress with simple flat sandals. After hesitating a few minutes, I took special care in choosing what I wore under the dress. Not that I was planning anything, necessarily, but it didn't hurt to be prepared. Lacy purple underwear and a matching bra never hurt anyone.

I dried my hair, thinking it was one of things I still had going for me. There wasn't even a hint of gray in the silky black strands. If I helped that out a bit once a month, it was at least one easy thing I could do to fight the onslaught of time.

As I finished doing my hair, a glint on my finger caught my eye. I glanced down at my left hand, where Daniel's rings remained. I had thought about taking them off at different points in the last year, but it had never felt right. And even now. . .I closed my fist and shook my head. Not yet.

I kept my makeup light, added a little perfume and was ready before I heard Logan's car pull into the driveway. Standing at the window, I watched him stride toward the porch.

He wore dark khaki cargo shorts and a plain green T-shirt.

I was surprised that he was dressed so casually, since I thought we were going out to dinner. When he got a little closer, I could see that he'd gotten his hair cut since I'd seen him in the morning. For some reason, that fact melted my heart just a little bit more. Yes, I'd been freaking out all day, thinking about tonight, but knowing Logan might have been worrying a little bit, too, made me feel so much better.

I opened the door before he could ring the bell, and Logan met my eyes with a smile. I had expected seeing him again to be awkward, uncomfortable, but Logan didn't pause. He stepped up to the threshold and slipped his arms around my waist. Before I could say a word, his mouth was over mine, possessive and warm.

He finished with a small kiss to the side of my mouth.

"Hi." He smiled down into my eyes. "I've been thinking about doing that all day. Waiting to get back to you and do that."

My mouth curved. "Hi." My heart pounding, I reached up and buried my hand in the back of his hair. Pulling him back to me, I kissed him again and felt his pleasure that I had taken the initiative.

Standing back, I gestured through the door. "Do you want to come in for a minute, or do we need to go? You didn't say where we were having dinner, so I hope this dress is okay."

"You're beautiful, as always." Logan brushed back my hair. "Perfect. We don't exactly have reservations, but I think we should head out."

I grabbed my handbag, locking the door behind us. Logan took my hand and led me to the car.

"So where are we going?" My curiosity got the better of me as Logan turned in his seat, backing out of the driveway.

He shot me a smile and wink. "It's a surprise. Do you trust me?"

"Of course, I do."

"Okay then." Logan turned down a side street. "Did you talk to Joseph today?"

"Yeah. Actually, I talked to both of the kids. Joseph sounded good. He's already totally in love with that baby."

"What about the baby's mom?" Logan glanced over at me.

"Not sure. He only had good things to say about her and her family. He's going to stay down there for a little while, I guess, and get to know the baby, talk with Lindsay about what comes next."

"I'm glad he seems to be handling it well. And you told Meggie? How did that go?"

"At first, she wanted to drive down to Clearwater herself and tell Joseph what an idiot he was. Her words, not mine. But she calmed down, and she's agreed to talk to him without screaming. So that's something."

"And how are you feeling about the whole thing?"

I sighed. "I know I wallowed in self-pity last night. But this morning, the more I think about it, and after talking to Sadie. . .well, it's not what I would have planned for him. And I know it's going to change his life forever, and nothing will be easy for him ever again. But in the grand scheme of things, he's not hurt or sick. He didn't break any laws. Once he found out about the baby, he did the right thing. So I guess I'm coming to terms with it, trying to see the happy."

I glanced around as Logan pulled into a small, nearly empty parking lot next to the beach.

"Logan, where are we going?"

"To dinner. I told you." He parked the car and turned to me. "Now, when we get out of the car, we're leaving Joseph and Meghan and the baby and everyone else in the world in here. We're not worrying about them for the rest of the night. Agreed?"

I frowned, but before I could say anything, Logan added, "It's not that I don't love them, too. You know I do. But you need a break from this, and I want you to relax. Plus—" He grinned. "I'll admit it. I'm selfish. I want all your attention, just this one night."

I laughed. "Okay, you got it. Not another word about the whole thing. But I have to admit, I'm a little lost."

Logan helped me out of the car. "How so?"

"I didn't know about any restaurant opening down here, and I know every hot dog stand in the Cove. Particularly if it's right on the beach."

"Ah." Logan twined his fingers with mine and brought our hands to his lips. He kissed my hand. "Did I say we were going to a restaurant?"

I cocked an eyebrow at him as we climbed over the small riser that bridged the dunes. To the right was a covered pavilion, and looking at it, I realized that it was decorated with draped material. Music played softly.

"Logan! What is this?"

We stepped down into the sand, and Logan tugged me closer, wrapping his arms around me. "This is dinner. Come on."

We made our way over to the wooden structure. A table was set up in the center, covered with a white tablecloth and flanked by two chairs. A cooler and tote sat off to the side.

Logan helped me on to the pavilion and slid out my chair. From the cooler, he pulled a bottle of wine and filled both glasses. He uncovered a cheese plate and a basket of bread.

"This is amazing." I looked around with wide eyes. "What made you think of it?"

Logan sipped his wine. "I remembered you saying once that going to a restaurant wasn't much fun for you, because all you could see was what they were doing wrong or how you would do it better. So I was thinking about takeout from a new place that opened near the office, but I didn't want to take it to your house or mine. Not tonight. And then I remembered this place."

"Good memories here." I glanced around. "And this cheese is delicious. What else do you have for me?"

Logan winked. "Guess you'll have to wait and see."

Chapter Sixteen

Jude

I HAD NO IDEA HOW LOGAN had pulled this off. The cold food—including cheeses, salads, a few different wines and butter for the delicious crusty bread—was chilled in the cooler, while the entrees and desserts were still toasty, wrapped in special heating towels within the tote.

"Oh, my God, Logan." I closed my eyes in bliss, savoring the short ribs that melted in my mouth. "This might be the best thing I've ever eaten. It's just fabulous."

He reached across the table to squeeze my hand. "Good. Want a bite of my sea bass?" He scooped a morsel onto his fork along with some couscous and held it in front of my lips.

"Mmmm." I smiled as I moaned in enjoyment. "Okay, now I can't say for sure which was better, yours or mine."

Logan's eyes darkened. "Keep making those noises, and we might not make it to dessert."

Heat flooded my center. I leaned forward. "We're not within walking distance of your house or mine. Or the Tide, even, for that matter. And as romantic as this is, the floor would be pretty hard."

"Jude, haven't you noticed how prepared I am here? Don't you think I've scoped out a secluded little spot in the dunes, behind the sea oats?"

When I stared at him, my lips slightly open, Logan laughed. "Have I shocked you? I'm just teasing. Well, mostly. I really am tempted to sneak off with a blanket, like everyone did back in high school during the dances."

I shook my head. "I never did that, and neither did you."

Logan quirked an eyebrow. "Don't you want to find out what we both were missing?"

"Not really. I know the beach is pretty quiet this time of year, but the idea of getting caught might. . ." I lowered my voice. "It might make me more inhibited." I leaned back in the chair, laying down my fork. "Not to mention the possibility of getting sand in some uncomfortable places."

Logan laughed. "Do you think that happened back in the day, with all those couples who came skulking back to the dances after rolling around on the beach?"

"I happen to know it did. Plus, sand fleas, other little critters. . ." I squirmed. "I guess I'm old and boring. When I have a perfectly lovely bed at home, just waiting—" I broke off, hearing my own words. Not that Logan hadn't made his intentions for this evening quite clear, but I didn't want to sound as though I expected him in my bed.

Logan picked up my empty plate along with his own and returned them to the tote. He pulled out two more covered plates.

"You've got to be kidding!" I held my stomach, laughing. "I can't eat another bite. Not yet, anyway."

"Okay." He replaced them and closed the tote. "Want to go for a walk then? Stretch your legs?"

I rose and gave him my hand. "That sounds perfect. Will all this stuff be okay here?"

"No one's going to bother it. And we won't go too far."

We left our shoes in the pavilion and walked toward the surf hand in hand. My heart beat a little faster as Logan's thumb caressed my palm between our entwined fingers.

"Last night—" he began.

"I want to tell you—" I said at the same moment.

We both laughed, and Logan tightened his grip. "Normally I would say, ladies first. But not right now." A small wave rushed up to cover our feet. "Last night was the most amazing experience of my life. I've been thinking about it all day. And I've been worrying, too."

I glanced up at him. "Worrying? Why?"

Logan pulled me closer, tucking me beneath his arm. I felt him take a deep breath. "Because falling in love with your best friend's wife—even when she's his widow—is tricky business."

If a rogue wave had suddenly risen over the beach and knocked me to the ground, I would have been less shocked. I stopped walking and stood with wide eyes, robbed of all breath.

"You really didn't know?" Logan tipped my chin up to look into my eyes. "Jude, we slept together last night. More importantly, I made love to you. It didn't occur to you that maybe it meant more than a romp in the sack?"

Almost unconsciously, I reached up and touched his cheek,

my fingertips tracing his jaw. "Romp in the sack? Logan, really. Of course, I didn't think that. But. . .love? That's just ..when? How long have you felt like this?"

Logan looked over my shoulder to the horizon. "Would it freak you out if I said I'd been in love with you for nearly thirty years?"

I jerked back, confused.

"I guess that's a yes." Logan caught my shoulders and pressed his lips to my forehead. "But don't. Jude, I had a crush on you years ago. But Daniel was my friend, and everyone knew you only had eyes for him. And he always belonged to you. So, yeah, maybe if things had been different, if you had a boyfriend who was a jerk, I would've made a move years ago. But you didn't. You were my best friend's girlfriend, and then my best friend's wife. So I made the decision not to be in love with you."

I frowned. "You made a decision? How do you do that? People don't decide who they love. It just happens."

"To a certain extent, yes. So maybe it's more accurate to say I made a decision not to act on that love."

I nodded slowly. "When did you change your mind?"

Logan kept his eyes leveled on mine. "I didn't think about it, Jude. It's not like after Daniel—after he was gone, that I thought, hot damn, I can go for Jude now. It didn't even cross my mind. All I wanted was to be there for you."

"When did it change?"

"I don't know, exactly. But one day you looked up me, laughing, and you took my breath away. I couldn't imagine living one day without you. And making you laugh again became my top priority."

I swallowed. "When were you going to tell me how you feel?"

Logan moved his hands from my shoulders up beneath my hair. He lowered his lips to cover my mouth, moving gently at first and then with more insistence. When he came up for air, he leaned his forehead against mine.

"I was going to do this." He spread his hand back to encompass the pavilion. "But I was going to do it before we did. . .what we did last night."

I looked down, toeing the sand around a shell fragment. "Are you sorry about what happened last night?"

"Hey." He nudged my eyes up. "No. Absolutely not. I'm sorry you were so upset, and I didn't mean to take advantage of that. But it was incredible, and I wouldn't change that for anything." He ran his hands down my back. "Are you sorry?"

It was something I had been deliberating all day, but in this moment, there was only one answer.

"No. I'm not sorry."

Relief flooded Logan's face, and he pulled me hard against him. The sun was tossing its final rays over the ocean as it sank on the other side of the world. The last beams danced over my hair until it gleamed like ebony.

A light breeze blew across the water, and in his arms, I shivered. Logan rubbed my bare arms.

"Let's go back up. I have a carafe of hot coffee."

It was nearly full-on dark as Logan seated me at the table again. He fumbled with something in the corner, and suddenly the pavilion was filled with twinkling white lights.

I gasped in pleasure. "Logan, it's beautiful! Did you do this?"

He shrugged. "It was my idea, but to be honest, I ran out of time. So I paid Karl—the kid who works for Matt—to come string them up. I'm glad you like it."

"I do." I smiled up at him as he set a mug of coffee in front of me. "You're full of surprises."

Logan grinned and reached beneath the table. The background music that had set the tone for dinner shifted, became louder. I recognized the opening strains of Madonna's voice as *Crazy For You* began to play.

Logan stood and offered me a hand. "Dance with me?"

I rose and let him pull me close. Just as he had in my kitchen a few weeks before, he wrapped one arm around my waist and held my other hand as we swayed.

"When we were dancing at the Tide the other night, this is what I wanted to do." With one finger beneath my chin, he tipped my lips toward his and kissed me. We moved side to side as he explored my mouth, taking his time and letting me set the pace. I met each stroke of his tongue with my own. Logan's hand moved up and down my back in sensuous circles before he brought it lower and pressed my hips to his.

He tore his mouth from mine to kiss his way to my ear, where he nipped lightly at the lobe.

"Would it weird you out if I told you that I always wanted to dance with you here? Do this on the dance floor?" He moved his hand to my breast, kissing me again, this time with less leisure and more passion. The thin cotton fabric of my sundress didn't hide much. I felt his fingers skimming all around the sensitive nub as his mouth left mine and traveled down my neck.

"No." I answered his question. "It doesn't. But you know, I never made out on the dance floor. I was too shy to do it with Daniel, in front of everyone."

Logan smiled and slipped his fingers beneath the top of my dress, found my nipple. He rolled it gently, and I sucked in a breath between my teeth.

I could feel evidence of his desire pressed at the juncture of my legs, and I began rethinking my objection to the secluded sand dunes.

"Logan." I kissed his ear, sucked the sensitive lobe into my mouth and was rewarded by his groan. "Logan. . .can we go somewhere? My house or yours? Please?"

"Mine is closer. Is that okay?"

"Closer is good."

Logan laughed, low and sensual.

"Let's go."

Chapter Seventeen

Jude

I HAD ALWAYS LOVED LOGAN'S HOUSE. Its open floor plan and walls of windows looking out onto the ocean felt like an extension of the beach, one that was protected from rain, from the sometimes-intense heat and from blowing sand.

Although I'd visited the house frequently while Daniel was alive, I hadn't been beyond the kitchen and great room since my first tour right after the house was built. It felt very strange to climb the steps to Logan's bedroom, following him as he held my hand.

The upper level of the house jutted out farther than the first floor, and with the wall of glass facing the beach, the bedroom gave the sensation of floating over the sand.

I walked to the windows and peered out into the velvet darkness. "Oh, Logan. This is so beautiful. Sometimes I forget how talented you are."

I turned, smiling. Logan had stopped at the top of the

stairs, where he stood staring at me, wearing an inscrutable expression.

"God, Jude. You're gorgeous."

I felt the heat rising in my face. "You make me blush more than anyone I've ever known."

He crossed to me, taking me into his arms. "Why is that, do you think? I only speak the truth."

"I think it's because you say things I never expected to hear from you. And it makes me feel . . ." I searched for the word. "Desired."

"You are. Very desired." He kissed my neck and then my lips. "And loved, too." He took a deep, steadying breath and squared his shoulders. "I said it before, but Jude, I want to be clear. I love you. I'm *in* love with you."

I searched his eyes, falling into the depths of the brown irises. Licking my lips, I laid a hand on his cheek.

"Logan, I have always loved you. Maybe in a different way than what you're saying, but I have. This is all happening so fast for me, and I need a little time to catch up to you. I don't want to say anything until I'm sure. Does that make sense?"

"Of course, it does." He brushed the hair off my forehead and framed my face. "I hope it doesn't mean you won't stay tonight."

I smiled and fit my body even closer to his. "I asked you to bring me to your house, didn't I? It wasn't to play pool."

He laughed. "I'm glad to hear that. Though I'm thinking a game of strip pool might not be out of the question."

His mouth swallowed my answer as he finally gave in to the overwhelming need. He opened my lips beneath his and tangled our tongues. I shifted to give him better access to my body and slipped my hands under his shirt. I ran my nails lightly over his back, humming in pleasure at the feel of his muscles.

"You know all those mornings you've come to drink my coffee?"

"Mmm hmmm. . ." Logan was distracted by my neck, tonguing the erratic pulse there.

"Did you realize I was ogling you every time you left?"

He straightened, smirking. "Really? So every time you were giving me a hard time about mooching off your coffee, you were thinking of this?" He grabbed my hands and moved them lower.

I laughed. "You've caught me." I found the hem of his shirt and tugged it upward. Logan stepped away just enough that I could take it off him. I rubbed my hands over his chest, as liquid heat settled lower within me, giving me the courage to let my lips follow my hands. I trailed my tongue over his pectorals and then on the flat discs of his nipples.

Logan growled between a clenched jaw. "Bed." He scooped me up in one fluid movement and dropped me on the king-sized mattress.

Giggling, I scooted toward the pillows. Logan unbuckled his belt, undid his shorts and kicked them off. Keeping his eyes fastened on me, he slid off his boxers as well.

My heart pounded, looking at him standing before me, lustful and unashamed. I swallowed hard, torn between the desire to reach for him and my inclination to dive beneath the covers of the bed.

He crawled onto the bed, smiling as he approached me.

"You look like a lion." I curled up close to the headboard. "Like a predator."

He laughed. "And you look entirely too dressed." He reached for the edge of my sundress, but I stopped his hand.

"Logan. . ." I bit my lip, trying to decide how to go on. "I'm not. . .you know, I'm not the same girl I was thirty years ago." I touched his chest, trailed my hand down his stomach. "I'm not in the same shape you are."

He brushed my hair back, nuzzled my collarbone. "Jude, I saw you last night. Has something changed since then?"

I shook my head. "Of course not. But you were—you know, we'd both had a lot to drink. And it was pretty dark. Plus, the heat of the moment—"

Logan moved the straps of my dress from my shoulders so that they hung on my arms, making the bodice sag tantalizingly between my breasts. "I hadn't had that much to drink. Not as much as you. And it might have been dark, but I have excellent night vision. There was plenty of heat, sure, but Jude. . ." He dipped his head low to plant a kiss on the top of my breast. "Believe me. You're beautiful."

He pulled the dress down the rest of the way to my waist and ran his lips over the soft skin that rose above my strapless bra. I closed my eyes and leaned back, sighing in pleasure.

Logan reached behind me and unclasped the bra, smiling in my eyes at the sight of my breasts in his hands. He took advantage of my pose—arms behind me, chest thrust into prominence—to pull a nipple into his mouth. He suckled, bit gently and then covered my other breast with his hand. When he moved to the other nipple, I moaned.

He kissed down the middle to my stomach, pausing only long enough to tongue my navel before he eased the dress the rest of the way off me, groaning when he saw the tiny purple lace of my panties.

"Are you trying to give me a heart attack?" He slipped a finger under the top and ran it back and forth, grinning up at me. "If I had known you were wearing these all night, no way we would have made it through dinner."

"Glad you like them." I fell back into the pillows and arched as Logan rubbed lower, covering the heat at my center with two fingers. He kept up steady pressure through the lace even as his mouth followed along. He used his teeth to drag the underwear down just enough above my knees. Hovering above, his fingers still moving within my folds, he looked up at me.

"Is this okay?" Without waiting for a definite answer, but going slow enough that he could stop if I wanted, he lowered his mouth to replace his fingers. I writhed and amped up my moan to a near-shriek as the sensation broke over me in a crashing wave. My breath came in small pants, my hands moving restlessly over his hair, until his tongue plunged within me.

"Logan!" I dug my nails into his shoulders, his name both a prayer and praise. He slowed his pace, kissing down my legs to my feet while I lay liquid, boneless, arms next to my head on the pillows.

When he joined me, one finger making circles up my torso to my breasts again, I turned my head and smiled. I raised one hand to snag his neck, drag him closer for a kiss designed to make him desperate.

When I pulled back a little, I kept my eyes open, on his, and moved my hand to touch him. Logan sucked in a breath.

I had never touched a man other than Daniel; we'd been together for so many years that our only experience was each other. Closing my hand around Logan's smooth hardness, a part of me still marveled at the fact that Logan wanted me, that I had elicited this response in him.

I held him tightly, moving up and down, my eyes never leaving his face. Pleasure was etched there; his eyes were closed, his mouth slightly open as he groaned. I rolled up onto my knees for an easier angle, but he caught my arm.

"I can't take much more." His voice was rough. "I need you, Jude. I need to be in you."

I slid onto him and kissed his chest. "I want you." I held his face between my hands and opened my mouth over his lips as he rolled me to my back. Without breaking the kiss, he raised himself over me and slid within.

We stopped for just a moment, our eyes locked. Logan smoothed my hair from my face.

"I love you, Jude."

I reached up, touched his cheek, raised my head for the most tender kiss I had ever known. I fell back again as he began to move, slowly at first and then faster, with more aggression.

My fingernails raked his back, and I arched up to meet every thrust. The pleasure built again to the point where I felt I had to let it go or I might shatter into a million pieces.

I half-screamed his name, tightening around Logan in pulsing spasms that undid him. He plunged into me one last time as every muscle in his body tensed and he roared my name.

He fell onto the bed next to me, rolling me with him so that our connection never broke.

We were quiet, not sleeping but content. Logan stroked my hair, ran his fingers through the strands.

"Logan?" My voice was muffled against his shoulder.

"Hmm?"

"Do we have to go back tonight and get all that stuff at the pavilion?"

He shook, and I knew he was laughing.

"No. I texted Karl on the way here, asked him to clean everything up and leave it on my deck."

I pulled back, eyes widening. "So he knew we were here? The whole time?"

Logan rubbed my back and pulled me closer. "No, of course not. Don't you trust me? I told him I was taking you home. My car is in the garage, so there's no way he could know that I meant I was taking you to *my* home, not yours."

"Ah." I relaxed again, looped my arm around his neck, shifting only slightly to let him kiss the pulse in my throat.

"So. . .does that mean dessert is downstairs on your deck?"

He propped up on his elbow to look down at me. "Do I take it you're hungry?"

I smiled. "I could use a little something sweet. I kind of worked up an appetite."

Logan chuckled and rolled over, breaking from me. He stretched once, reaching up as his body became one large quiver. He jumped from the bed, unabashedly nude, and reached over to give my rump a light smack.

"If it's food you want, it's food you'll get. Besides, you need to hydrate and fuel up for round two."

"Round two?" My eyes were round as I watched him disappear into the bathroom. I flopped back onto the pillow and laughed. Life was so strange. Here I was, a grandmother of all things, having mad sex with the hottest man I knew. In my wildest dreams, I never would have imagined myself here, doing. . .this.

I hopped up from the bed and followed Logan, eyes dancing.

"Logan!" I called. "Could round two include ice cream?"

Chapter Eighteen

Jude

I MADE TO THE TIDE IT in time for opening the next morning, but I wasn't alone.

"Driving here with you is so much better than running down on the beach," Logan observed. "Not that you're not worth it."

I slid him a sideways glance. "Aha. So this sudden passion for running in the early mornings wasn't about my coffee, was it?"

He moved his hand off the steering wheel to squeeze mine. "I love your coffee, but it was more about seeing you."

I laughed and then had to stifle a yawn. "You know, I'm going to be totally worthless today. And what am I going to say when Sadie and Mack ask where my car is?"

"Here's a thought. Tell them the truth."

"Oh, okay. I can hear it now. 'Sadie, my car is still at home in my garage because I spent last night with Logan at his house, having the most mind-blowing sex of my life. Over and over again. And then he insisted on driving me to my house so I could get clothes for today, and while we were there, he jumped my bones again.' Yeah, that's going to go over well."

We rolled to a stop sign, and Logan turned toward me, eyebrows raised. "The most mind-blowing sex of your life? Really?" The grin on his face couldn't have been any smugger.

I rolled my eyes. "That *would* be the one part you heard."

"You could just say I gave you a ride this morning. Let her draw her own conclusions."

"Her own conclusions wouldn't be much different than what I just said." I leaned my head back on the seat as Logan pulled into the parking lot. When he took the keys from the ignition, I swiveled my eyes toward him.

"You know it's not that I'm ashamed of anything we did, right? I'm not trying to hide it. It's just going to take some time for me to get used to the idea."

Logan leaned across and brushed his lips over my mouth. "I know. It's going to be weird at first, but we'll get through it."

"Part of me wants to keep it quiet because. . .it feels good to have something that's just ours. But I know realistically that doesn't work in the Cove, let alone with. . .oh, my God, Logan! The posse. What are they going to say?"

Logan glanced away. "They'll be fine. They want you to be happy, Jude. They're our friends."

"I know you're right, but still. Don't you think they'll be a little surprised? A little shocked?"

Shrugging, Logan climbed out of the car. "We'll cross that bridge. Too early to think about it this morning."

It was oddly comfortable to have Logan with me as I

unlocked the door. I was used to meeting him at the restaurant each morning, but walking in together, having spent the night in his arms, offered a different level of intimacy.

"This is nice." I went through my normal routine while Logan made coffee. "If I had known how good you were at opening a restaurant, I might have hired you years ago to take over for me."

"About that." Logan turned and leaned against the counter. "I was thinking. Have you considered hiring someone to open for you a few mornings a week?"

I frowned. "No. Why would I?"

He tugged me flush to his body and kissed me. "Because I'm not as young as I used to be, and after a night of mind-blowing sex, to quote you, I might not always want to get up at the crack of dawn. And I'm damned sure not staying in bed while you come in and do it, so get that thought right out of your head."

I pulled away and stuck my tongue at him over my shoulder. "But this is my thing. I always open the Tide."

"Yep, I know. But things can change, Jude. You and I are living examples. I'm not asking you to turn your life upside for me, but wouldn't it be nice to travel a little? Spend a week in Napa? Or go to Italy?"

I took out the eggs and tilted my head, considering. "I've wanted to do that. I always thought eventually I would. Daniel and I—" I broke off and turned my back to Logan.

"Hey." He rubbed my shoulder. "Don't do that. You never worried about bringing up Daniel in front of me before. Don't do it now."

"I feel. . .I don't know. Kind of funny. Not like I'm cheating on him, though I thought I might feel that way. But like it would be easier for you if we pretended I didn't have a past."

"Jude, if it weren't for Daniel, you and I wouldn't have each other. I'm grateful to him. He's still my best friend, and he's still your first love. Nothing is going to take him away, and it shouldn't."

Tears filled my eyes, and I smiled through them. "Thanks. I needed to hear that."

"I want us to talk about him. Hell, if I know Daniel, he's grinning now. At the very least, I think given everything else, he'd give us his blessing."

"I hope so. I know he wanted me to be happy. He told me that. But I told him there wasn't ever going to be another love for me." I twisted to look up at Logan again. "Do you think that makes me a liar?"

He kissed the tip of my nose. "No, I think that makes you human. What else would you say? And when your husband is dying, I would think the last thing you want to think about is starting over."

"True." I wiped off the counter next to the range. "You know what I said a little bit ago? About the most mind-blowing sex of my life? That wasn't just to inflate your ego, you know." I bit my lip and leaned against the fridge. "Daniel and I had a wonderful life. And things in that area were really terrific." I met Logan's eyes. "We'd been together for so long, so many years. There were rough times, sure, but in the last few years, with the kids grown and so many pressures off, it was really good."

He nodded.

"But last night was incredible, Logan. Feeling wanted again

was amazing. Feeling desirable. And feeling that way with someone who has been like a best friend to me for so long, too—it
was icing on the cake."

Logan grinned. "Don't you mean whipped cream on my—"

"Stop!" I swatted his arm as the blush crept up my face. He
caught my hand and pulled me close again, pausing for just a
moment to look into my eyes before he kissed me thoroughly.

We were lost in the kiss, in each other, when I heard a loud
throat clearing, and Sadie's voice rang out from across the room.

"What's that you're doing in my kitchen?"

We jerked apart, more out of surprise than anything else.
Mack stood back, his face pink and embarrassed humor in
his eyes. Sadie, on the other hand, looked from me to Logan
expectantly.

"Well? Which of you is going to tell me what's happening here?"

Logan leaned down to drop one more kiss on my lips. "As
much as I'd love to stay and fill you in, I need to get to work. I
missed a lot of time yesterday." He rounded the bar and kissed
Sadie's cheek as he passed her, and then clapped Mack on the
shoulder.

"Good luck, man."

I busied myself whipping eggs in the large bowl. "Everything
is ready. I think the coffee's done. You want me to make you up
a cup?" I couldn't quite meet Sadie's eyes.

"Mack, take this rag and go wipe down the deck tables."
The older woman snagged a towel from the hook.

"But I thought I'd have some coffee."

"Get going. I'll make it up and bring some out to you."

Grumbling all the way, Mack took the rag and went outside.

"Now you." Sadie came into the kitchen and crossed her arms over her chest. "You have something you need to tell me?"

"Hmm?" I wondered if playing dumb would buy me any time at all. Good God, where were my normal early bird diners? Anyone who might distract this old woman, who had been a second mother to me and had now fixed me with beady eyes.

"How long has it been going on?"

I gave up. "Not long. Just—the night before last. He came in right after Joseph left, to make sure I was okay. And I had a little limoncello, and then . . . well, you know what they say. One thing led to another. . ."

"Is it serious? Or are you two—what do they call it now? Friends with benefits?"

"Sadie!" I shook my head in shock. "Where do you pick up this stuff? No. Well, not really. I mean, we're still friends, but it's more than benefits." I twisted the edge of my shirt between my fingers. "Sadie, he says he loves me. That he's in love with me."

For the second time in two days, Sadie's eyes filled with tears. She pressed her lips together and nodded. For a moment, neither of us spoke, and then Sadie patted my arm.

"Honey, no one deserves it more. And I hope he realizes it. I've known both of you since you were gangly young things. I love you both. So I hope you make each other happy."

She sniffled and yanked a paper towel from the rack to blow her nose loudly. "Now look what you've done. You've got me bawling again, like a crazy old woman. We've got no time for this. Give me those eggs, and you take that dotty old man outside a mug of coffee before he drops."

I felt all day as though I was floating. Sadie and Mack seemed to have called some kind of truce, either in deference to me or maybe even inspired by romance in the air. I hid a smile when I spied Mack pinching his wife's backside as he passed her. Love, young, old or somewhere in-between, was a beautiful thing.

We had a steady flow of customers, but nothing so challenging that it distracted me from my memories of the night before. A few of my regulars commented that they were glad I seemed to be feeling better.

"You've been looking a little peaked, honey," remarked one of the crusty old fishermen who stopped for beer in the early afternoon, after being up and out on the water since before dawn. "But today you looked all perked up. Got you a nice little glow."

I smiled and patted his shoulder. "Thanks, Ernie. Aren't you a sweet one?"

The cell phone I always kept in my back pocket buzzed, and I smiled when I pulled it out, seeing Logan's name on the screen.

"Do you miss me?" I asked, slipping out onto the deck, where it was quiet and empty.

"You know it." His voice was husky. "How is your day so far?"

"Good." I stepped into the sunshine and tipped back my face to feel the warmth. "How about you?"

"Excellent. How could a day that began like mine did be anything but?"

I laughed. "Okay. So . . . what's up? Or is this—what would Sadie call it, a booty call?"

"I wish. No, I forgot to tell you that I got word from the"

contractor, the B and B is ready for a walk-through. If everything's a go, we can begin having the furniture brought in this weekend. Right on schedule for opening in two weeks."

"Oh, that's great, Logan." I turned in the direction of the sunny yellow house as though I could see it through the Tide. "When do you want to do it?"

"I thought we could meet there after work and go through it then. I'll make you dinner after, if you want. Either at my house or yours."

The idea of having someone to plan with, to be accountable to again, made me smile.

"That would be perfect. What time?"

"Will five-thirty work? I can be there by then, and Emmy takes over at five tonight, right?"

"Yup, sounds good." I turned to lean against the railing of the deck. "I'll see you then."

"Okay. I love you."

He hung up before I could reply. Standing above the beach, feeling the salt air and hearing the roar of the sea, I was once again a teenager, hugging a phone to my chest and dreaming of the boy I loved.

Because I did love Logan. I had been sure of it, almost from the first time he'd kissed me only two nights before, but it hadn't sunk in until this morning in the kitchen, when he had spoken of Daniel, of him always being part of our lives. It struck me then that I could never love someone who didn't accept that Daniel would always be in my heart. We had shared decades, a marriage, children, a life and a death. Nothing could destroy that, and ignoring it would be somehow cheapening what we had.

Thinking of my children, I realized that Logan and I still had a few hurdles to jump. We had to break the news not only to Meghan and Joseph, but to our own friends, as well. We had to tell the posse about us before someone else did.

Joseph called later that afternoon to check in, tell me more about Lindsay and what a terrific mother she was, and how smart and beautiful their baby was. I listened and put in a word here and there, but I didn't say anything about Logan. There would be time, and it was something I preferred to do in person, after Joseph had recovered a little from his last big shock. These few days had been an emotional ride. Though I could see the blessings now, my heart was still a little tender.

After we hung up, Joseph texted me pictures. When I saw the one of my son holding *his* son, I couldn't help it. I sat down and burst into tears.

Chapter Nineteen

Jude

THE COVE WAS A SMALL town, and news traveled at lightning speed. I knew I had a limited time before the word about Joseph being a dad made the rounds; whispers about my relationship with Logan wouldn't be far behind. We had to act fast to tell our friends and my kids before they all heard it from another source.

I was relieved that Emmy seemed blissfully ignorant of everything when she arrived that Friday night. The younger woman didn't seem to notice anything amiss with my hurry to leave, either, especially since I had the ready excuse of the walk-through at the bed and breakfast.

"I can't wait for it to open," Emmy said as I gathered my handbag and made a final check of the kitchen. "I'm already having fun putting together the pastry selection for the breakfast menu."

Contracting with Emmy to supply our pastries and desserts had been an easy decision. I liked keeping everything within my little business family, and Emmy had proven herself both talented and trustworthy.

I thought about it with satisfaction as I walked up the street. Logan's car was already on the curb in front of the house, and I spied him stepping around the side, examining something on one of the porch railings. I saw he had discarded the suit jacket he'd worn in the office, and the sleeves of his white shirt were rolled to the elbow. A shot of pure lust ran down my middle, and I smiled, knowing I could satisfy that need in just a few hours.

The wide and welcoming porch was one of my favorite parts of the old house, and one I had insisted we keep when re-designing it. Climbing the steps, I ran one hand over the gleaming white banister and brushed a foot across the blond oak floor. It was perfect, just as I had envisioned.

"Hey, beautiful." Logan had come up behind me in stealth mode. He put his hands to my hips and kissed my cheek. I wondered if the same thoughts about discretion until we shared the news had crossed his mind, or whether he was just acting in deference to us standing on the corner of what was for all purposes the town's main street.

"Hi." I reached behind and gave his hand a quick squeeze. "Sorry I was late. I tried to get down as soon as I could."

"I'm early. I wanted a chance to check some of the little issues that cropped up during building, make sure they'd been addressed. They had," he added, in answer to my questioning look. "Everything looks good structurally. The landscaping in the back is coming along nicely."

We walked inside, and I oohed over the spacious foyer

with its brass wall sconces. The chandelier in the dining room glittered, and the addition of a bay window in what had been a formal parlor—and would henceforth be a cozy sitting room—was perfect.

Cooper had made the new banister that accented the staircase based on Daniel's ideas and suggestions. I touched it, remembering conversations we'd had about it. I could almost hear Daniel's voice, and I smiled.

Logan covered my hand as it lay on the dark wood.

"You can feel him here, can't you?" He looked back down the steps at the rooms below us and then glanced ahead. "This was his baby. He was so excited about it. He wouldn't miss the walk-through."

I smiled and nodded, and we continued up to the bedrooms. Each room was unique, with special windows or a certain type of closet. The bathrooms were small, but they all had been updated with the most modern amenities.

"Remember what Daniel used to say? 'People like to look at old stuff, but not when they're in the shower.'" I giggled, thinking about it.

Logan laughed, too. "Nice thing is, we were able to incorporate some fixtures that look like antiques, but have modern functionality." He pointed to a claw-footed tub that sat within a black and white bathroom. "The plumber retrofitted that to make it work in here. Old tub, all new faucets, pipes and trim."

"It's beautiful." We were safely upstairs, completely alone, and I turned to step into Logan's arms. "You should be very proud, Logan. You and Daniel had a vision, and you've made it come to life. I can't wait to see it filled with people."

He held me tight and rested his chin atop my head. "First comes furniture, then come the people. Abby sent me an update on reservations today. We're filled solid for the first month, and there's a steady stream of bookings rolling in still."

I turned within his embrace, resting my back against Logan's chest, looking into the fading twilight.

"When does the sign go up?" We'd ordered a simple white shingle to hang on the porch.

"That'll be the last thing. Cooper's having his guy do the lettering. I wanted to talk to you about the name. I know we always said we were going to call it the Holt Hawthorne House, but I think I'd like to change that."

"Oh?" I swiveled my head back to look at him.

"I was thinking of making it just Hawthorne House. In honor of Daniel. And if you're okay with it, I'd like to hang his portrait in the sitting room."

I smiled. "I'm very okay with that. I like it. And so would he."

"I think you're right."

I bit my lip, hesitating to bring up something that had been on my mind for the last few days. "We talk about Daniel all the time. But I was thinking the other day about Tess. You came very close to marrying her, Logan. Did you love her?"

I felt his arms tighten around my waist. "Tess was. . .she was a beautiful person, inside and out. I needed someone to take my mind off you, off what you and Daniel had together. She knew, somehow. But she was okay with it. She told me there were different kinds of love, and she thought the two of us could make a life together, be happy."

"I remember how hard it was when you lost her."

He nodded. "I decided then, I think, that I wasn't going to settle again. It wasn't fair to the other person. I felt a lot of guilt over Tess, and it took a while to move beyond that."

I touched my lips to his. "If you need to talk about her, I don't mind. Like you said, it's silly to pretend people we love didn't exist."

He held my face with one hand and kissed me with lazy passion.

We stood for a few moments soaking in the ambience of the house. Through the window, I could see the town. Lights were coming on in all the businesses on Beach Street; everyone stayed open later on Friday nights. If I craned my neck, I could even see the Rip Tide. People strolled on the sidewalk, kids hung out in groups outside the ice cream parlor, and tourists window shopped.

"Logan?" I shifted a little, lay my head on his chest.

"Hmm?"

"We need to tell the posse. And Meggie and Joseph. People are going to start to talk, and I don't want to hurt anyone by letting them hear about us from anyone *but* us. That is. . ." I leaned back to see his face. "That is, if there's something to tell. I don't want to pressure you into calling this something it isn't or make you feel trapped—"

"Jude." He held my face and kissed me, tracing his tongue over my lips before coming up for air. "I thought I expressed this clearly last night. I love you. If I didn't think it would totally freak you out, I would be begging you for a commitment, to move in together. To plan our life. And I'm not going to wait long for that, because I don't want to waste a minute. So, yes, I agree with you about telling everyone. I thought maybe we'd have another one of your Sunday dinners, only this time at my house instead of the Tide. What do you think? I'll make some calls tonight, make it happen."

"I think that sounds like a great idea. I don't know about Meggie and Joseph. I'm more worried about them than the others, but I think it would be better to tell them in person."

"Joseph will be home soon, once he figures out how to deal with having a kid. And if he brings that baby up here, you can bet Meggie will be down. Let's give it some time."

"Okay." I stood on tiptoe and brushed his lips. "Where are we going to eat tonight? Your place or mine?"

We ended up at my house, where Logan grilled steak and baked a few potatoes. My contribution was a green salad and a bottle of wine I opened for us to share.

We ate on the back porch, alongside the pool, enjoying the peace and each other.

"I wasn't sure if you'd want to come here," I remarked, scooping up a bite of potato with sour cream. "Before last night, I mean. I thought there might be too much of Daniel here."

Logan shook his head. "No, not at all. Remember last night on the beach, you're the one who said we should go the closest house. And that just happened to be mine."

"Time was of the essence. I was. . .eager."

"Yes, you were." Logan mock-leered and grinned.

"Well, I'm glad you don't mind being here."

"I don't. But that being said. . ." He laid his knife across the edge of the plate. "Have you given any thought to what you want to do with the house?"

"Do with it? Well, I live here."

"Yes, I know. But I'm hoping that pretty soon, we won't need two houses. And eventually, we should talk about which one makes more sense for us to keep."

I toyed with a piece of lettuce. "I can't think of that yet. I'm just getting used to the idea that we're in love. Thinking about moving in together will have to wait until next weekend."

I expected Logan to protest, but instead, his lips curved into a smile, and his eyes were bright. "So we're in love?"

I cocked my head. "Didn't we have this discussion already?"

"No. I said *I* was in love with you. *You* said you needed time."

"I did? Well, that was then. I took the time I needed. And now I'm telling you that I'm in love with you, too." I paused, considering. "I guess there was a more romantic way to handle that, wasn't there?"

"Nope. That was totally Jude. And as long as you're telling me that *we* are in love, together, you can say it any way you like."

Chapter Twenty

Logan

I WAS NERVOUS.

I hadn't expected nerves over this. In my mind, telling Jude how I felt, trying to convince her that the two of us together was not only a good idea but meant to be was going to be the hard part. But now we had to share with the most important people in our lives that we were in love. Even knowing that it wasn't going to come as much of a surprise to the posse didn't relieve my anxiety.

And of course, that was another cause for worry. I knew Jude was a reasonable person, but I didn't think it was wise to confess the posse's plan to woo her. Women were funny about those kinds of things.

I spent half of Saturday working on business I'd let go over the course of the week, making telephone calls and meeting with Abby, the woman we'd hired to run the bed and breakfast for us. She was an experienced hotel manager in her early thirties, pretty with dark hair and wide brown eyes. As we chatted,

I thought about Cooper, the lone unattached member of the posse now that Matt was dating Sandra and I was with Jude.

"Hey, are you busy tomorrow afternoon?" My words were an abrupt change of subject, and the surprise showed in Abby's eyes.

"Ah. . ." She cast her eyes up and ran a tongue over her lips. "Well, no. I mean, I was thinking of hitting the beach if the weather holds, but if you need me to do something, I can absolutely cover it."

"No, not work. I'm having a bunch of my friends over to barbecue and hang out. Since you're new to the Cove and you'll be working with some of these people, it might be a good time for you to meet them."

Abby shifted in her chair. "Sure, I can do that."

"I should probably warn you, though, that I have an ulterior motive for planning this for tomorrow."

Abby looked at me with a frown, and I thought I even detected worry. "Oh, really? What's that?"

"Well, can you keep a secret? At least until tomorrow? Jude and I are. . .together. And we're telling our friends tomorrow."

Abby leaned back in her chair, smiling. "That's wonderful. Congratulations. Jude is a terrific person. I haven't gotten to know her very well yet, but I've been down to eat at The Rip Tide a few times, and she's always so nice."

I felt the stupid grin that spread across my face, but I couldn't help it. "She's great. This wasn't anything we planned, you know, and it's still kind of new, but. . ." I spread my hands in front of me. "I've never been happier in my life."

Abby laughed. "Well, that's good to hear. I have to confess, when you started talking about tomorrow, I was afraid—God, this is going to sound conceited. But I thought you were about to ask me out."

I stared for a minute. "I'm sorry, Abby. I didn't mean to give you that impression. I mean, you're, umm, very nice, and pretty—"

"Stop!" Abby shook her head, still laughing. "I'm relieved. Not that you aren't attractive, but I'm just not looking for that in my life right now."

"No? That's a shame. Lots of good men in the Cove."

Abby smiled. "I appreciate that, but for the time being, I'm focused on my work. No offense to you, but I've decided men are too much time, energy and work."

I stood up and gathered the papers we'd been discussing. "Do me a favor, and don't tell Jude that, okay? I've got her fooled so far into thinking that being with me is actually a good thing." I winked at Abby.

"You got it, boss."

I left the bed and breakfast and made my way down the sidewalk toward the Tide. I stopped at The Surf Line to say hello to Matt.

"Hey, Mr. Holt!" Karl stood behind the counter, grinning broadly. "How you doing?"

"I'm good, Karl. Thanks. Is Matt around?"

"Nah. He took a couple of guys out on a fishing charter early this morning, and they're not back yet."

"Okay. Tell him I stopped by, would you? No reason, just to say hey."

"Sure." Karl cocked an eyebrow. "Did everything go okay the other night? With Miss Jude?"

I shot the boy a stern look. "That's between the two of us, right? You didn't say anything to Matt?"

"Me?" Karl looked wounded. "I told you I wouldn't tell Mr. Spencer. And I didn't."

"Good man." I smiled. "I knew I could count on you. Don't worry, we're going to tell everyone tomorrow. But I appreciate your help."

I swung back out onto the sidewalk and headed to the Tide.

Jude was working behind the bar, and for a moment, I stood just within the doorway and watched her. A couple of old fishermen sat on stools, hunched over mugs of beer, and she was laughing with them. I thought of all the times I'd had to avert my eyes from Jude's smile or risk betraying my own feelings by the expression on my face. Knowing that I didn't have to hide anymore was exhilarating.

I sauntered into the restaurant. Jude caught sight of me right away, and her face brightened.

"Watch out, gentlemen," she said, leaning toward the fishermen. "Here comes trouble."

I walked around the bar and kissed her cheek. I paused just long enough to whisper in her ear.

"If it were tomorrow already, and we'd told the world, I'd show you just how much trouble I am."

I was rewarded by her blush as she shook her head and rolled her eyes. The two men watching poked each other with their elbows and snickered.

"You two, behave." Jude pointed at them both in turn. "Or

I'll cut you off and tell your wives you come and sit here for an hour instead of coming right home every day."

They had the good grace to look abashed. The taller man laid his hand over his heart and looked up at Jude with wide eyes.

"As if we ever do anything less than behave! Come in here every day only to support the local business. Just like we did with your dad."

His companion nodded with the same self-righteous expression. "It's that boy there you want to be watching." He gestured toward me. "I see the look in his eyes. He's up to no good!"

Jude leaned her elbows on the bar and set her chin in her hands. "I think you might be onto something. What's your advice?" She tossed a smile of challenge at me over her shoulder.

"Eh." The first man waved one hand. "Keep him close, so you can make sure he's doing as he ought. Don't let him get away with anything."

"Nah, you got it wrong." His friend shook his head. "Toss him back and take me instead." He offered Jude a beatific smile, displaying a number of missing teeth.

I raised my my and backed away, wagging my head. "Okay, boys, I concede defeat. She's all yours." I lowered his voice and added, "Just be warned. She might be a little too much woman for you." I raised my eyebrows meaningfully, and the men hooted.

Jude tossed down her rag and turned toward the kitchen. "That's it. You're all on your own. I give up."

I followed her into the back and cornered her next to the

fridge, where we were mostly hidden from the rest of the room. I pulled her tight to me, my hands molding her backside.

"Did you miss me?"

Jude linked her hands behind my back and looked up at me. "Miss you? Have you been somewhere?"

I kissed her once, just a light touch of lips. "Brat. I've been slaving away all morning, catching up on work that I should have done this week when I was being your sex slave."

"Shh!" Jude peered around me. "Someone will hear you and think you're serious."

"And I'm not?"

She shot me a look and ducked beneath my arm. "Everything go okay with Abby?"

"Yeah. We scheduled all the shipments, and she's meeting with Emmy and our other suppliers this week. Everything's on track for opening day."

"Wonderful." Jude began breading chicken tenders and dropping them into the deep fryer.

"Oh, hey, guess what? Abby thought I was asking her out."

Jude stopped and cast me a look. "What? Why?"

"I invited her to my house tomorrow, and she thought it was like a date. I had to tell her the truth."

Jude smothered a sigh. I knew she was realizing that it was becoming less and less likely that she could keep her kids from hearing about her new relationship from someone other than their mom.

"So is she coming?"

"I think so. Don't you think Cooper would like her?"

Jude moved to the sink to wash her hands. "Cooper? I don't know. They've met, haven't they?"

"Yeah, but Cooper. . ." I trailed off. Telling Jude that Cooper had been saving himself for her wasn't something I was ready do. "That was through work. It would be different if they met with all of us, just hanging out."

"Logan Holt, are you turning into a matchmaker?" Her eyes dancing, Jude tilted her head at me. "After all the teasing you gave me about Matt and Sandra? Could it be?"

"No." I shook my head. "No. Hell, no. I just thought they might like each other, is all." I scowled at her.

Jude just smiled at me, saying nothing.

I heaved a sigh. "If I'm just going to get harassed, I'm going home." I stomped past her, stopped and wheeled around.

"See you tonight," I said, so low she could only just hear me. "I'll have dinner ready when you get there." I brushed my lips over the top of her hair. "I love you."

"Bye!" Jude called across the room as I left. "Try to keep some of those arrows in your quiver, Cupid!"

I stopped at the door, turned and shot her a rude gesture before stalking out, leaving her bent over, dissolved in laughter.

Chapter Twenty-One

Jude

I KEPT BUSY ALL DAY SUNDAY and tried not to worry about the evening. I loved my friends. I was confident in their love for me. But I wasn't certain what this new relationship would mean to the dynamic of the group.

At five o'clock, I turned the sign over on the door to the Rip Tide and locked up. Since Logan had driven me to work that morning, I'd asked Emmy for a ride to his house.

The red mini-van sitting in the parking lot was an old model, but it was carefully maintained, the way all of Emmy's possessions were. I climbed into the front passenger seat and turned around to say hello to the kids...who weren't in the back.

"Where are the kiddos?" I pulled on my seatbelt and looked at Emmy.

"My parents took them to the mountains this weekend, up to Georgia. Totally spontaneous grandkids and grandparents' weekend. Wish I'd known earlier. I might have planned something fun."

"Ha!" I shook my head. "No, you would have booked some extra work for the weekend."

"True." Emmy pulled out and slid a sideways glance at me. "So. . .not that I mind at all, but you want to tell me why I'm giving you a ride to Logan's house? You having car problems?"

"No." I knew that Emmy's curiosity would get the best of her, and I had already decided I wouldn't lie if asked. "Logan drove me to the Tide this morning."

Emmy was silent for a beat. "Why did Logan drive you to work?"

I licked my lips. "Because I slept at his house last night."

Emmy braked at a red light and turned in her seat. "Are you going to make me pull this out of you, or are you going to come clean with me?"

I expelled a breath. *Look at this as a dress rehearsal for telling everyone else*, I thought.

"Logan and I are. . .involved." I chose the word with care. "We've been seeing each other. And he invited everyone over tonight so we can tell you all."

"What does 'involved' mean?" Emmy's tone was neutral.

"God, Emmy, what do you think it means?"

"I hope it means you're having hot and dirty sex with that gorgeous man."

I felt the red creeping up my neck. "Nice, Emmy."

"Well? Is that a yes?"

I closed my eyes and nodded. "Yes."

"Yahoo!" Emmy thrust her hand in the air. "I am so happy for you and so totally jealous. Not of Logan," she added hastily. "Just of the hot and dirty sex."

"And here I was hoping we could keep this whole thing on a higher plane. You know, talk about love and all that. Old friends who grow to be more."

"Love? Did you guys already use the 'L' word?" Emmy pulled into Logan's driveway and grabbed my arm. "So this isn't just, you know, a physical thing?"

"You mean friends with benefits? That's what Sadie said." I rolled my eyes.

"Sadie knows? You told her before you told me?"

"I didn't tell her so much as she caught us. In the bar."

Emmy threw back her head and laughed. "Whooo, boy. I would've paid money to see that. What did she say?"

"She's happy for us. She said we both deserved a chance at happiness."

Emmy laid a hand on my arm and squeezed lightly. "And that's what we're all going to say. I couldn't think of two people who deserve it more. A second chance at love." She sighed.

"I know." I leaned my head back and closed my eyes. "I can't really believe it. When Daniel died, I thought that was it. I figured that part of my life was over. No one is more surprised than me that I'm in love again. And with Logan."

"Every time you say love, I want to cry." Emmy sniffed a little. "He loves you, and you love him...I'm so glad for you, Jude." She opened her car door and grinned at me. "Now we get to go in and tell everyone else."

I groaned. "Just make sure I get a glass of wine the minute I walk through the door. I'm going to need it."

The door to Logan's house was unlocked, and I could hear

noise coming from the back. Taking a deep breath, I followed the sounds.

The great room flowed into the multi-level deck through a wall of sliding glass doors. All of them were pushed open, as was the door to what the other women and I referred to as the Posse Cave. I spied Logan at the massive grill on the deck, head back as he took a swig of his beer. At the sight of him, standing legs wide, laughing at something Eric was saying, a possessive wave of lust swept over me.

"Look at you." Emmy stood at my side, murmuring. "You're totally smitten."

I didn't deny it. She just smiled.

"There she is!" My brother Mark jumped up from where he was sitting at the kitchen counter. He hugged me. "We were starting to think you'd blown us off."

I kissed his cheek. "I'm not late. It's not even five-thirty yet."

"Yeah, but the rest of us have been here all afternoon."

I snorted. "Some of us work for a living, brother of mine. Seven days a week."

"Mark, leave your sister alone and let her into the kitchen. We need another hand." Samantha gave her husband a gentle shove. "Go outside with your little friends and let us cook."

I followed Sam back behind the counter as Emmy wandered out onto the deck. "What can I do?"

"Not a thing. That was just me rescuing you from Mark. You've been on your feet all day, I bet. Sit down. Want a glass of wine?"

I glanced out at the grill, where Emmy was now chatting

with Logan. "Sure, wine sounds perfect. Are you positive I can't help?"

"Nope, we've got it covered. Sandra is doing the baked beans, Janet's got the salad, and Logan is handling the meat." She set the tall glass of Sauvignon Blanc in front me, lowering her voice. "Any movement on the Logan front?"

"Ahh. . ." I stalled. "I'll tell you later, okay?"

Sam cocked her head. "Sure. You all right?"

"It's been an interesting few days." I sipped the wine, closed my eyes and hummed in appreciation. "This is so good."

"It is, indeed. We're just about ready to eat, I think." Samantha shot out her arm and snagged her son as he tried to run past. "Hey, you. Go tell Uncle Logan we're all set in here. He can bring in the meat. And—" She stopped him one more time when he tried to squirm free. "Be sure you stay and help him bring it in."

"*Okay*, Mom." He skidded away before she could hold him up any longer. Sam sighed.

"Boys." She set a stack paper plates and a basket of plastic ware on the end of the counter. "Logan said he wanted to make a toast once we were all here, before we eat. So I'll set us up, and then we can dig in when he's done. You know anything about that? The toast?"

I shrugged, and my stomach rolled a bit. Logan and I hadn't talked about how we were going to make this big announcement, but I had assumed it would be something quiet, casual. Mentioning it to a few of our friends, letting word spread through the party. Apparently, he had a different idea.

Logan came in, carrying the platter of hamburgers. His eyes

met mine, and there was a certain joy there, a peace I'd never seen in him. He winked subtly, and deep inside me, something that had been teetering on the brink of completion fell into place.

This was right, Logan and me. No matter how our friends reacted, or what my children said . . . we were good together, and nothing could change that. We were meant to be.

Logan set down the burgers and turned to scan the room. The rest of the guys were making their way inside, and the kids clamored to get to the front of the food line.

I made an instant decision. I climbed off the stool and maneuvered my way across the room until I reached his side. His attention distracted by something Matt was saying, he didn't see me until I slipped my hand into his.

When he turned his face to smile at me, I reached up my other hand to cup his cheek, drawing his lips down to mine. Our mouths met in a kiss that was intimate, aggressive and promising.

All around us, conversation ground to a halt.

Logan brought his arms around me, meshing our bodies. One hand rubbed slow circles on my back.

I eased away, ending the kiss. Logan still held me, even as I turned within his arms to look at our friends.

Logan cleared his throat. "So. . .I don't have a drink to raise a toast, but I can make one anyway. Jude kind of stole my thunder. We're together. Jude and me. This isn't something temporary, and we're not—" He glanced to where Sadie sat on the sofa. "—friends with benefits. We're friends who now just happen to be in love."

In the kitchen, Janet gasped, and Samantha sniffled. The men shifted on their feet, looking around at each other.

Cooper was the first to speak. He stepped toward Logan and me, throwing an arm around the two of us.

"I'm happy for you both." He glanced around the room. "We all are." There was a murmur of consensus—at least, I hoped it was consensus. "But let's get to the important stuff. Is it finally time to eat?"

The laughter broke any tension, and everyone streamed toward the food. Logan stood where he was, holding me. We watched our friends find places to sit, juggling plates my full cups.

"Are you hungry?" Logan's hands, crossed in front of me, tightened on her hips as he spoke low by my ear.

"Mmm." I turned my head to shoot him a suggestive smile. "But food would be good, too."

"Are you relived now that we've told them?"

I lifted one shoulder. "Mostly. It was kind of weird, don't you think? The guys didn't seem very surprised. Janet, yes, and Sam and I had talked a little before, but Cooper didn't. And look at my brother! He's just sitting there, eating."

Logan found my hand, linked our fingers. "Maybe people see more than we give them credit for?"

"I guess. We need to tell them all that the kids don't know yet. And, crap, Logan, I need to tell them about Joseph."

"Yes, you do. Or we do. But I thought that was more of a one-on-one thing."

"Good idea. Speaking of which . . . until Samantha said something, I didn't know you were going to use a toast to break the news of us."

Logan grinned at me. "You do know I was just going to raise a glass to good friends, both here and no longer with us, right? I was surprised when you came over and kissed me, but then I figured I had to say something."

"Oh." I closed my eyes. "Sorry. I thought—and then I just decided to take action. I should have trusted your plan."

"Yeah. Hey, do you see that? Abby's sitting with Cooper. I told you they'd get along."

"You're so smart." I kissed his cheek and wriggled away. "I'm going to grab a plate before the burgers are gone, and then I'll go do some talking."

Telling my friends that I was an unexpected grandmother turned out to be the bigger news of the day. Eric and Matt were angry with Joseph at first. They asked me questions about paternity tests and timing, and I found myself defending a girl I had never met.

By the time I returned to the kitchen to help with clean up, I was exhausted.

"But you haven't told Meggie and Joseph yet?" Janet was drying dishes as I washed.

"No. I want to talk to them in person. It's happened so fast, Janet."

"Mmm." Janet pursed her lips and put away another pot. "Too fast?"

"No, I don't think so." I rinsed my hands one last time and dried them. "I can see it might seem that way to you, but it's not like we had to get to know each other, go on all those awkward first dates. . .we're friends."

Mark wandered over to us. I noticed a sway in his gait and thought he might have had a little more to drink than normal.

This suspicion was borne out when he flung an arm around my shoulders.

"I'm happy for you, Jude. Really happy."

I might have been touched if not for the slur in his words.

"Thanks. I hope you remember that when you're sober."

Mark either did not hear me or chose to ignore what I said. "I'm glad it was Logan, you know? I thought, but I wasn't sure. It might have been Cooper. He's been married lots, I know, but still. Or Matt, even. Why not? You have a lot in common."

I hung the towel over the oven handle. "Why did you think I'd be with any of them, Mark? I wasn't exactly trolling for men."

"No, but the pact. It had to be one of them, right? So we can take care of you. So you don't ever leave the Cove."

Janet frowned and glanced at me. Samantha came into the kitchen. "What's going on? Mark, what did you say?"

"I told Jude about I was glad it was Logan who won. That's all."

"Won? What are talking about?"

Some sense of self-preservation dawned in Mark. "Nothing. I just—I think I had a few too many beers." He tried to grin.

I looked across the room to where Logan was talking with Eric and Matt. He looked up, met my eyes and smiled. An assurance I couldn't quite explain radiated from within me, and a sense of peace filled my heart.

"Never mind, Mark." I stood on her toes and kissed my brother's cheek. "I'm glad it was Logan, too."

Chapter Twenty-Two

Logan

STANDING AT THE DOOR THAT night, waving goodbye to the last of our guests, I decided this was one of my favorite parts of being in a relationship with Jude.

"Do you know how great this is?" I rested against the door jam and grinned down at her as she leaned against my chest. I held one of her hands in mine.

"Watching everyone leave, finally? Yeah, I can see that." Her smile was tired, and I wrapped my arms around her waist and closed the front door, shutting out the night.

"You must be dead on your feet, working all day and then dealing with this." I moved the silken black hair off her neck and kissed her there. "But no, that's not what I was talking about. I mean, having you stay with me after everyone else leaves. I always hated how empty my house felt when you all went home."

I turned her toward me and tipped her head up, kissing her lips. "Doesn't feel empty tonight. So thank you."

She snaked her arms around my waist and sighed, laying

her head over my heart. "You're welcome, and thank *you* right back." She snuggled into me and rested for a minute.

"I think it went well tonight." I led her back into the kitchen where I turned off the lights. "Ready for bed?"

"More than." But she didn't move toward the steps. "Janet asked me if this—you and me—happened too fast."

"What did you say?"

"I told her no. I said that we had the advantage of knowing each other already, so once we knew there was something more than friendship, moving into love felt exactly right."

I kissed the back of her hand. "That's beautiful, and it's true. It might feel fast to some people, but I've been falling in love with you by degrees for thirty years. That's quite a courtship."

Jude followed me up the stairs. She was quiet, and I wondered if she missed being home. We'd spent every night together since Thursday, and I knew she was used to a certain amount of alone time.

"Jude, you know, you have to tell me if you're feeling overwhelmed. If you need a night by yourself, it won't hurt my feelings."

She flashed me a smile as she kicked off her shoes in the bedroom. "Are you trying to get rid of me already?"

I crushed her to me and growled into her ear. "Not hardly. I had trouble not dragging you up here tonight while all our friends were still hanging around. I don't know if you can understand." I kissed down her neck onto her shoulder, nipping lightly at the muscle there. "Just seeing you in my house, walking around. . .feeling like you belong here. . .it's so freaking hot.

I've never had that. So I'll never get enough. You have to tell me if it gets to be too much."

Jude ran her hands down my back, moving lower until she covered my rear end. She pulled me tighter, closing her eyes as she felt my desire for her evidenced.

"Not too much yet." She released me and stepped back to peel off her T-shirt. I disappeared into the bathroom to brush my teeth.

"Mark was a little worse for the wear tonight." Jude raised her voice to be heard over the running water. "How many beers did he have?"

I turned off the water and answered around my toothbrush, wandering back into the bedroom.

"I don't know. I wasn't keeping track. You worried about him?"

"No." Jude unbuttoned her shorts and slid them down to her ankles. Picking them up, she stood as though debating for a moment. So far, I'd noticed, she'd been taking her dirty clothes home to wash. She eyed the wicker hamper inside the door of my closet, seemed to make a command decision and chucked her clothes into the basket with mine.

"Hey, who does your laundry?" In just her bra and underwear, she followed me into the bathroom as I went back to the sink.

I rinsed my toothbrush and glanced at her. "Me. Why?"

"Oh. Well, I know you have a housekeeper, I wasn't sure if she did your wash, too." She joined me at the sink and retrieved her toiletry bag. "I just put my clothes in your hamper, so I'll do a few loads, too."

"Wow, you're the best roommate ever." I walked behind her and patted her ass. "I take it back. You can never leave."

Jude brushed her teeth, washed and moisturized her face. When she came back into the bedroom, I was lying on the bed, arms crossed behind my head, wearing just my boxers, checking email on my phone. I smiled as she came closer to me.

She sat on the edge of the bed, rubbing cream into her legs. "Mark said something kind of weird tonight. I just chalked it up to a few too many beers."

My eyes flicked across the phone screen. "Oh, yeah? What did he say?"

"Something about how he was glad I chose you. That it could've been Matt or Cooper. And he mentioned a pact." She re-capped the lotion, set it on the nightstand and swung her legs onto the bed. "Do you know anything about that?"

I set down my phone. "Do you really want to know?"

Jude sighed. "I'm guessing you'd like me to say no, but yes, I do. Does this have something to do with Daniel?"

I looked up at the ceiling, praying that telling Jude the truth wouldn't change anything between us.

"No—but then again, yes. It was the night after we spread his ashes. We were all here, and we'd been drinking for a while." I drew a deep breath. "Someone mentioned you and how hard everything had been for you. Daniel's illness, then losing him. And we all talked about how you were still young, and maybe someone would come into town and you'd fall in love and leave the Cove. Leave us."

I turned my eyes toward her face. "I don't remember exactly how it got to that, but someone said maybe it would be better if it were one of us. You could fall in love with Cooper, Matt or me. We said we'd let you choose. All of us would kind of date you, and then see what happened. And no hard feelings, no matter how it turned out."

Jude was very still. Her eyes were fastened on the center of the bed, and I couldn't read her reaction at all.

"But see, here's what they didn't know. I already knew I was in love with you. I didn't tell them, because. . .hell, because we'd just really said goodbye to Daniel. I know it had been a year, but that day was final. I guess part of me felt like what the guys were suggesting gave me permission to act on what I felt. Do you understand what I mean?"

For a full moment, Jude didn't move at all. When her eyes finally met mine, I saw humor. Relief flooded my body.

"So that's why Matt took me out to dinner and tried to wine and dine me? And why Cooper kissed me and tried to flirt?" She shook her head, eyes rolling. "Logan, what would you have done if I'd given either of them any encouragement? What if one of them felt something for me more than obligation and friendship?"

I reached toward her, just touching her fingertips where they lay on the bed. "I guess I would have fought them for you. I kind of almost did, a few weeks ago."

Jude cocked her head. "Explanation, please?"

"Cooper told us he'd kissed you. I sort of lost it. I thought I'd moved too slow, missed my chance."

Heaving a sigh, Jude flopped onto her side, cradling her head in the crook of her elbow. "Dangerous little game you were playing there, dude!"

I leaned over her, my breath tickling her cheek. "You were worth it. And it doesn't matter, does it? Because I won." I lowered my lips to hollow in her neck, to the dip that intrigued me.

Jude smiled. "You're awfully sure of yourself."

"Shouldn't I be?" My answering grin was cocky. I leaned back just enough to watch her. I watched an intriguing gleam dawn in her eyes.

Pushing up on her hand, she shoved me onto my back and sat over me, one hand lightly in the center of me chest to hold me still.

My mouth curved into a wolfish smile. "Finally got me where you want me, huh?"

She threw her leg over me, straddling my body with both hands now resting on my chest. "Maybe I do."

She bent over and feathered kisses on my cheeks, down my neck and onto my chest. She ran her lips around my pecs and circled her tongue around the flat nipples. I pulled in a hissing breath.

"You're killing me."

"Am I?" She spoke against the center of my chest and then wriggled lower, licking along my abs. "Driving you crazy?"

"Hell, yes." I threw back my head as Jude moved ever lower. She kissed along the top of my boxers, shifted so that she rode my thigh and pulled off the boxers. Dropping them to the side of the bed, she turned back to grasp my erection with both hands, smiling at the rumble of pleasure in my chest.

Jude lay over me, stroking me and writhing against my leg.

"Want to be crazier?" she murmured, and without waiting for an answer, took me in her mouth.

I groaned. Encouraged, Jude circled me with her tongue, laved and suckled. Her cheeks hollowed as she moved up and down, each touch of her hot mouth making me more insane.

"Jude." My hands were in her hair. "I want—"

She released me and crawled back up my body, raining kisses along the way. She found my ear, nibbled the lobe for a minute before whispering again.

"You want?"

She rose up, centered her body on mine and sank onto me, arching at the feel of me deep within her. I grasped her waist as I moved her up and down. Jude rode me, increasing in speed until I shouted her name, my body a quivering mass of muscle. My surge triggered her own release, and she fell on top of my chest, breathless.

"Jude?" I lifted my head just enough kiss her forehead. "Have I mentioned that I'm madly in love with you?"

She nodded against my chest. "You might have said something about it." She turned her head so that her chin rested on my sternum. "Is there anything else you need to tell me about the posse and pacts? Better tell me now while I'm feeling. . ." She quirked an eyebrow. "Generous."

"Nope. When I almost hit Cooper, I sort of confessed that I was in love with you. So they all backed off. That's why the guys weren't that surprised today."

"I noticed that." Jude snuggled back down, laying her ear so that she heard the steady beat of my heart. "I've known the posse for a long time, Logan. I love them like my brothers. But I'm only *in* love with one of them. I won't ever ask you to betray

178

secrets about the guys or not hang out with them. Just remember, though, that I need to come first."

I lifted her so that her eyes were level with mine. I kissed her on the mouth and leaned her forehead against mine.

"First, last and everything in between. Always."

Chapter Twenty-Three

Jude

EARLY FALL WAS MY FAVORITE time in the Cove. The beaches were less crowded during the week, and I felt like I had a moment to breathe between breakfast rush and the lunch crowd. And it was a good thing, because it turned out that my newly complicated life was taking up a lot of time.

My days began to fall into a rhythm. Logan drove me to the Tide each morning, had his coffee as I prepared for opening before he headed to his office. He usually checked in with me by telephone at noon, and then returned at five to pick me up. He made sure that we spent some nights at my house, and slowly some of his clothes moved over to my bedroom, just as my makeup and books found spots at his home.

Joseph called me one Wednesday morning not too long after we'd come out to the posse. He was still in Clearwater; while I was slightly anxious about the classes he was missing, I was glad that he was having time with the baby.

When I answered the phone, his voice was filled with excitement.

"Mom? How would you like to meet your grandson?"

I was flipping a burger, and I nearly dropped it. "Of course! When? Are you coming home?"

"I thought Lindsay, DJ and I would drive up there tomorrow, if that's okay. Can we stay with you for the weekend? I talked to Meggie, and she's going to drive down on Friday."

"Absolutely." I began making plans. "Does Lindsay have a travel crib, or do you want me to get one? What else do you need?"

Joseph laughed. "Lindsay says not to worry. She has everything under control. Wait, hold on." I heard a muffled conversation on the other side of the phone.

"She says if you have a crib, that would be great. Otherwise, we can work out everything else."

"Wonderful. What time do you think you'll be here?"

"I'm not sure. I'll text you along the way. Traveling with the baby takes a lot longer, you know. We have to pull off the road for Lindsay to nurse him, and he needs to be changed, like, every hour, sometimes." I smiled at the new tone of parental confidence in my son's voice, after only a short time of fatherhood.

"I'll wait to hear from you, then. If you get in earlier, I can have Sadie and Mack cover the Tide for me."

"Cool." He paused for a moment before adding, "Mom, I can't wait for you to meet Lindsay and DJ. I know you're going to love them both."

I spent that night cleaning my house, paying special attention to Joseph's room.

"Do you think he and Lindsay will sleep in the same room?" Logan and I sat on the floor, putting together the pack and play I'd bought that afternoon.

"I don't know." Logan shrugged. "I mean, asking them not to is kind of like barring the barn door after the horse got out, right?"

"Maybe. I was thinking that it would hypocritical for me to enforce that rule, given that my bed isn't exactly lonely these days."

Logan laughed. "Guess you've got a point. But you know, I'm willing to be very discreet while your kids are at home. And I'll give you all the space you need."

I reached across to pat his leg. "I really don't want any space. I want you to be with me when I tell them about us. It's not like I'm bringing some stranger into their lives. Meggie and Joseph already know you, and they love you, too."

"Still, it's one thing to love me as Uncle Logan, and another to accept me in their mother's life."

That conversation stayed in the forefront of my mind the next day. I jumped every time my phone buzzed, though I knew the kids had gotten a late start from Clearwater. I figured I would have time to close up and head home before they arrived.

Only one customer sat at the bar when the door opened just before four. Sadie and I were working in the kitchen, wiping down counters and putting away food in preparation for closing. Hearing the tinkling bell, I frowned. I had hoped this person eating at the bar would be the final customer for the day.

"I just hope this one doesn't want a burger. I just scraped the grill," I muttered to Sadie, drying my hands on my shorts as I stretched my back. Sadie didn't answer, because she was standing stock-still in the middle of the kitchen.

I followed her gaze and saw my son on the other side of the bar, holding his baby boy.

I flew around the counter to grab them both into a hug. "Is this any way to sneak up on a grandmother? You said you'd text!"

Joseph laughed. "DJ slept the last part of the drive, and we made better time than I thought we would. I knew you'd be here, so we just decided to surprise you." He laid the blinking baby in my arms. "Mom, this is Daniel Joseph."

"Ohh. . ." I choked back tears as I gazed down at the wide blue eyes. "He's so beautiful." I touched his dark hair, his plump baby cheeks and the tip of his perfect nose. I was so completely absorbed that it took me a moment to notice the girl standing next to Joseph, biting her lip and looking supremely uncomfortable.

"You must be Lindsay." I turned to her with a smile and opened my free arm to offer a hug. "Welcome to Crystal Cove. I'm so happy to see you again."

"Thanks, Mrs. Hawthorne." Lindsay returned the hug.

"Please, call me Jude." I cuddled the baby and then glanced up his mother. "He's just perfect, Lindsay. Thank you for bringing him here, so I could meet him."

"Hey, I did the driving!" Joseph shook his head in mock affront, but he put his arm around Lindsay, squeezing her shoulders.

Sadie approached us. "Boy, what's the matter with you, coming in here and not introducing your young lady to Mack and me?" She swatted the back of his head in her familiar affectionate way.

Joseph grabbed the older woman in a bear hug and spun her around. "Sadie, this is Lindsay. Linds, this gorgeous woman is my first love. She used to sneak me sweets when I was little and Mom was working."

"Nice to meet you." Sadie nodded, but her eyes were glued on the baby. "Jude, stop being such a hog and give me that little one."

We passed the baby around, with even Mack coming out to take a turn and admire him.

Finally, I shooed Joseph and Lindsay to the door. "You must be exhausted. Joseph, take them home. Everything is set up in your room for the baby, and you know to help yourself to whatever you need. I'll be along in about twenty minutes."

"Nonsense!" Sadie shook her head. "Mack and I can handle closing. You ride home with the kids."

"Yeah, Mom, where's your car?" Curiosity tinged Joseph's voice. "I almost thought you weren't here when we pulled in and I didn't see it."

"Ah, Uncle Logan drove me in this morning." I avoided meeting my son's eyes and turned to Sadie. "Are you sure you're okay here?"

"Don't be ridiculous. Get going." Sadie shooed us out.

I climbed into the back next to the baby's car seat. As Joseph and Lindsay buckled him in, I pulled out my phone and texted Logan the update in plans.

As soon as we arrived home, Lindsay ducked into Joseph's bedroom to nurse the baby. Joseph carried in several loads of baby necessities and began to put them away. I changed and headed for the kitchen to start dinner.

Joseph sat at the table, staring at the glass of water in front of him. He smiled at me as I came in.

"I was just sitting here thinking how much I miss Dad." His voice was thick, and I laid a hand on his shoulder.

"I know. I miss him, too. Every day." I pulled out the chair to sit down across from her son.

"Mom." Something in his voice made me wary. "I know you miss Dad. But is something going on with you and Uncle Logan?"

I leaned back in my chair and heaved a breath. "Why do you ask?"

"Since when does anyone drive you to the Tide for opening? And when I went to put some of the baby's clothes into the washer, I found a load still in there. And there were boxer shorts among your . . ." His face reddened. "Your *stuff*."

I nodded. "Yes. I was going to tell you, but we were going to wait for dinner, tell you together. I'm sorry."

Joseph stared at me. "Mom. . .are you sure? And is this serious, or are you just messing around?"

I leaned forward, smiling. "It is kind of serious, sweetie. And am I sure? Yes."

"But if you're just lonely or need. . ." Joseph shook his head, clearly deciding not to go down a road he didn't want to consider. "Why?"

"Because we're in love. I know you probably don't want to think about that, but it's the truth. Not while Dad was alive," I hastened to add. "This doesn't have anything to do with your father, other than that Uncle Logan and I both loved him, and we always will. I don't know how these things work. I don't know why I've been given this second chance, but if there's one thing I learned in the last two years, it's that life is short. You take it with both hands when it's offered to you."

"I'm not mad at you, Mom. I'm just kind of shocked. I guess I thought after Dad, there wouldn't be anyone else. But if there has to be, I'm glad it's Uncle Logan."

"He's a very good man." I smiled, relief filtering into my mind.

"Are you going to marry him?" Joseph's voice was neutral.

"I don't know, honey. I won't say no, but we haven't made any definite plans."

"Does Meggie know?"

I shook my head. "Not yet. I figured I'd tell her this weekend." I grinned at my son. "What a family we are! Never a dull moment, huh?"

"Not lately." He fiddled with the glass in front of him. "Mom, do you like Lindsay?"

"I really do. She seems like a sweet girl, a wonderful mother."

"She is." He took a deep breath. "I think we might get married."

I wasn't shocked, but I nodded slowly. "Are you sure that's the right thing for both of you? And for the baby?"

He spread his hands on the table. "Yeah. Pretty sure. I thought I might be in love with her before all this. And now, I'm certain of it."

"I want you to think about it long and hard, both of you.

If you're positive, then I'll support you a hundred percent. How do Lindsay's parents feel about the idea?"

"After they met me, and we all got to know each other, they were all for it."

"That's good." I paused and bit my lip. "Joseph, I put the baby's crib in your room, but I wasn't sure what your sleeping arrangements would be."

My son smiled. "We'll both sleep in my room so we can be there for the baby, but I promise, that's all we'll be doing. Lindsay's parents talked to me a long time about what they believe, and Lindsay feels the same way. We might have started out on the wrong foot, but we're going to wait now until we're sure. Until we're married."

His mouth raised in a half-grin. "But Mom, I really can't wait for that wedding."

Chapter Twenty-Four

Logan

"**W**ELL, THAT WENT BETTER THAN I expected."

I was loading the dishwasher as Jude wiped down counters and the table. "I have to cop to some nerves on my way over here. But Joseph seemed pretty comfortable with the whole situation."

"He is, I think. He was a little surprised at first, but he pulled it together." Jude folded the towel and leaned a hip against the fridge. "Lindsay seems nice, doesn't she?"

"Yeah. She'll keep Joseph on his toes, I'd say, but if the way he looks at her is any indication, he won't mind."

"It's sweet, isn't it?" She smiled. "But let's talk about the most important thing. How adorable is my grandson?"

"He is absolutely the cutest baby I've ever seen." I closed the dishwasher and turned to grab Jude by the waist, backing her against the counter. "How could he not be with a nana like you?"

Jude looked up at me. "And you were so good with him.

188

He loved you." She toyed with a button on my shirt. "Does it bother you? Not having kids, I mean? Choosing me definitely means shutting that door."

"There is no choice, my love. Besides, I get to share Meggie and Joseph, and I also get a piece of that little guy. Assuming you'll stop being so greedy with him." I swatted her behind and headed for the coffee pot.

"Very funny. So, are you going to miss me tonight?"

I poured some coffee for both of us and sat down at the table. "You know I am. I'm still not entirely clear on why I can't stay if Joseph doesn't object."

"It's not so much for Joseph as for Lindsay. She and Joseph have made a commitment to wait on being together until they get married—if they get married. I respect that, and I don't want to make her uncomfortable."

"I have to admit, I'm impressed by them. I'm not sure I could have done the same thing at their age."

"Daniel and I did." Jude sipped from her mug.

"Really?"

"Yes. Why do you think we got married before he finished college?" She glanced at me. "Daniel never told you that?"

"No. Contrary to what you might think, men don't always sit around talking about their sex lives." I considered what I'd just said and then added, "Much, anyway."

Jude laughed. "Okay, then. Now you know. We . . . fooled around a little bit, of course, but my parents were pretty strict, you know. I lived in terror of getting pregnant." She shrugged. "I had friends who couldn't understand it, but I knew that Daniel was the man I wanted, and he knew I was the one for him. We held out . . . well, until we just couldn't anymore, and that's when we decided we couldn't wait for him to graduate to get married. His parents were very unhappy, but in the end, it wasn't their decision."

"Did you ever regret it?" I thought I knew the answer, but I had to ask.

"Never." She smiled and sipped her coffee. "But as much as it might make me a hypocrite now, since I'm having sex outside marriage on the regular, I want to respect Lindsay's feelings on the matter."

"I understand." I leaned back. "Just means we'll have time to make up for later."

"True." She sighed, resting her chin in one hand. "Are you coming to pick me up in the morning? Or do you want to sleep in? I'll be fine."

"Nope, you're not getting rid of me that easily. I'll be here at the crack of—well, dark. And then I'm taking Joseph to lunch."

"I heard that. He's going to drop Lindsay and DJ off at the Tide before he meets you. I get to show them off to all my customers."

"When do we expect Meghan?"

Jude winced a little. "Probably after dinner. I'm a little more worried about her than I was about Joseph. He's in a place where showing grace is easy, because he needs it, too. But Meggie. . .she was a daddy's girl. And she can be a little rigid. I'm really not sure how she's going to react."

190

Jude

That worry about Meghan stayed with me through the next day, even as I enjoyed the time with Lindsay and DJ.

"Do you know you're the sixth generation of my family to be in this restaurant?" I bounced the baby on my hip.

"Really? That is so cool." Lindsay sat at a nearby table. "I love this place. And Joseph walked us around the town today. It's perfect."

"The Cove is pretty amazing." I perched on the edge of a chair and turned the baby around, laying him on my knees so I could look into his eyes. They were blue, which of course could change one day, but for now, he had Daniel's eyes.

"Lindsay, I know this isn't the way you probably planned to start a family. But I want to thank you, not only for this sweet boy, but for not giving up so easily on my son. And what you named the baby. . ." I kissed his chubby bare feet. "It means so much."

"It was an honor." Lindsay reached across to touch the baby's soft head. "It wasn't easy, when I found out he was coming. I didn't know until after. . .well, Joseph was already gone. I went home, and my parents were devastated. But once they came around, I had lots of support. It wasn't that I didn't want Joseph involved. I wasn't trying to hide the baby from him. But I figured he was dealing with enough. If I had it to over again, maybe I would do it differently. But I always wanted DJ to know his dad. And all of you, too."

"Thank you." I buried my face in the folds of DJ's neck and

nuzzled. "Oh, little man, what am I going to do with you on the other side of the state?"

"Just as I suspected." Logan approached. "You leave a woman with another man, and when you come back, she's kissing his neck."

I looked up, laughing. "Sorry, Logan. You're just going to have to accept that you now have competition."

Joseph leaned down to kiss Lindsay's cheek. "Are you ready for me to drive you and the baby back to Mom's house? I thought you might both want a nap before my sister arrives."

"Sounds like a good idea." Lindsay stood up, and with regret, I handed the sleepy baby over to his mama. "Thanks for lunch, Jude. See you tonight."

"Get some rest, all of you." I watched the little family leave, and a sense of contentment settled over me. They were going to be okay, I thought. It wouldn't be easy, but I was fairly confident in their future.

Logan sat down on a barstool, watching me as I rose to my feet.

"Don't you have to go back to work?" I began bussing a table.

"No, I had cleared the afternoon for lunch with Joseph. I'll catch up on a few things tomorrow. Where are Sadie and Mack?"

"Mack had a doctor's appointment, so I told them to take the afternoon off. I had to practically force Sadie to go with him. How was lunch?"

"Interesting. I was impressed with how much Joseph already has thought this whole situation through. He has some good ideas for their future."

"Really? That's good to hear." I carried the dishes into the kitchen. "You want a beer? It's Friday, you're done work. And I'm positive it's five o'clock somewhere."

"If you're offering, sure." Logan watched me reach under the bar, come up with the bottle and pop the top.

When I began to slide it across the bar to him, he shook his head. "I think I need a more personal delivery."

"Oh, you do, do you?" I smirked as I came back around the bar and stood in front of him with the bottle. "Does the delivery girl get a tip?"

"I think it would only be right." He pulled me between his legs, angled his head and took possession of my mouth. He sucked my lower lip and then tangled his tongue with mine.

I looped my arms around his neck. "I take it you missed me last night?"

"Mom?"

I jerked back, nearly knocking Logan off the barstool. Across the room, just inside the open door, stood Meghan.

I scrambled to get to my daughter. "Meggie! You're early. I didn't expect you until after dinner." I pulled her into a hug, conscious that she wasn't returning the embrace.

"My last class was canceled." Meghan kept her voice neutral. "Uncle Logan?"

"Hi, Meggie." He didn't move from the stool.

"What's going on?" She turned toward me. "Were you *kissing* Uncle Logan?"

"I. . ." I turned to look at Logan. He shrugged.

"Yes, Meghan. I was kissing Uncle Logan. We—we're seeing each other." I shot him a look, and he smiled in encouragement.

193

Meghan's mouth dropped open. "Seeing each other? What does that mean?"

"Meghan, you're almost twenty-two years old. I think you know what it means."

"I can't believe this." She hitched the backpack higher on her shoulder. "How could you let this happen?"

"It's not something we 'let' happen. It's something we've chosen."

"But what about Daddy? How can you—he hasn't even been gone two years, and you're already forgetting about him? Moving on with life?"

I glanced from Logan to my daughter, distress making my voice quiver. "No one's forgetting your father, Meghan. I loved him with all my heart. I still do. But he's not here anymore, and I know for sure he'd never want me to stop living."

Meghan swung to face Logan. "And you? His best friend? How long did you wait before you pounced on her?"

"There was no pouncing, Meggie." He kept his voice calm. "Your mother and I—we didn't plan this. But that doesn't mean it isn't right."

My daughter looked down, her mouth tight. "I can't deal with this right now. I'm going home. Is Joseph there?"

"Yes, he just headed back there with Lindsay and DJ. Give me a minute to close up, and Logan and I will go home with you."

"No." She turned back to the door. "I want to go now. I'll see you there later." She stomped out the door.

I sighed and slumped against the bar. "That did not go well."

Logan folded me into his arms. "I'm sorry, Jude. You're

right—I think we took her by surprise, and she didn't exactly handle it gracefully." He kissed the side of my head. "But try not to let her get to you. She just needs a little time. She'll adjust."

∼⊙

Logan

Jude's daughter had not adjusted by the time Jude and I got back to her house, nor did things get any better as the evening went on. Dinner was a stiff and tense meal, so different than the night before. Meghan seemed to love the baby, but she was cool to Lindsay, bordered on rude to me and barely spoke two words to her mother.

The next morning, Jude cried all the way to the Tide. Driving the car, I felt more helpless than I ever had in my life.

After I left the restaurant, I turned back to Jude's house and let myself into the kitchen. It was still quiet, but Lindsay sat at the kitchen table, holding the baby.

"Good morning," she said, keeping her voice low.

"Everyone else still asleep?" I poured my second cup of coffee that morning.

Lindsay nodded. "The baby was awake a few times last night, and Joseph insisted on getting up with him. So I thought I'd let him sleep in a little this morning."

"That was nice of you." I cast my eyes upward. "And Meghan?"

She shook her head. "Haven't seen her."

I sat across the table, watching this pretty young girl with

195

the drowsy baby on her lap. "You know it's nothing personal, Lindsay. With Meggie, I mean. She's not a bad person. Just someone who's had to deal with more than her fair share of upheaval and loss this year."

Lindsay smiled. "Oh, thanks, Logan. I'm not worried about it. I have three sisters. There's not much someone like Meghan can do to really get under my skin."

"That's a very mature way to look at it." I took another swig of coffee. "I had a good talk with Joseph yesterday at lunch. He's pretty determined that you two should get married, the sooner the better. How do you feel about that?"

Lindsay cheeks went pink. "I guess I'd say I'm on the same page." She shifted the baby in her arms, touching his cheek. "It must seem really fast to you and Jude in some ways. But Joseph and I were getting serious last year before he left. I know a lot happened in between then and now, but. . ." She looked down at the baby. "I still love him. I never stopped."

I cleared my throat. "I can relate to that. A lot of people might say Jude and I are moving fast, too. Some *have* said it. But I guess when you know, really know you're with the person you love, waiting around doesn't make much sense."

"That's it exactly." The baby gurgled, and Lindsay laughed. "DJ agrees."

I grinned. "You and I have a lot in common right now. We're both coming into this family at a time when they're still healing. It isn't always going to be easy. If you ever need someone to talk to, don't hesitate." I set down my mug, toying with the handle. "I appreciate how Joseph is handling everything with his mom and me."

Lindsay shrugged. "He was a little rattled about it when we first got back here and he suspected something was going on. But we talked about it. I reminded him we weren't exactly poster children for doing things the easy way."

"I thought you might have had something to do with that. Thanks, Lindsay."

There was a sound outside the kitchen, and Meghan appeared from around the corner, wearing sweats that ended at the knee and a huge green T-shirt. She stopped short at the sight of Lindsay and me.

"Good morning." I held up my mug. "Want some coffee? Your mom made it before she left, so it's safe to drink."

Meghan lounged against the doorway. "What are you doing here? You sleep here, too?" Behind the insolent tone, I heard pain.

"No," I answered evenly. "I slept at my house. Came by to pick up your mom and drive her to work, and then came back here. To talk to you."

Meggie snorted and shoved off the wall. "Well, here I am. So talk."

Lindsay pushed back her chair. "I think someone needs his diaper changed." She cast a sympathetic look at me as she slipped past Meghan.

"Sit down, Meggie." When she remained across the kitchen with her arms crossed, I rolled my eyes. "Meghan, you're almost twenty-two years old. Start acting like it. Sit down so we can talk like grown-ups."

With a heavy sigh that I guessed was supposed to

indicate long-suffering, Meghan scraped back the chair and dropped into it.

I picked up my mug and filled it before pulling out a clean cup. I doctored both coffees and set one before the sulking girl at the end of the table.

We sat in silence for a few moments, with Meghan refusing to meet my eyes.

I gritted my teeth. She wasn't going to make this easy on me. Part of me wanted to walk away, let Meggie figure it out for herself. But then I remembered Jude's tears in the car that morning, and my resolve strengthened.

"Meghan, I've known you since the day you were born. I was at the Tide with your mom and dad the day she went into labor, and I went to the hospital with them. Outside of your parents and the doctor, I was the first one to see your face. And since that day, I've loved you like my own."

Meggie kept her eyes down on the table, but I detected a quiver in her bottom lip.

"Your father was my best friend, bar none. All of us in the posse love each other like brothers, you know that. But we all have closer connections, too. Mark and Cooper hang out. Daniel and I were buds from elementary school. When we were in middle school, my mom walked out on our family. Daniel kept me from freaking out. He took me home for dinner every night for a year. He made sure I was okay."

I wondered if Meghan had heard this before. I never talked about my family, and I doubted Daniel had mentioned it. I saw her swallow hard.

"You mom and dad were together from the time we

started high school. Even before then, we all knew they had something special. Jude had stars in her eyes when she looked at Daniel, and Daniel just plain never saw anyone else.

"I'm going to be honest with you, Meggie. I had a crush on your mom in those days, too. If Daniel hadn't been there first, no question I would have chased her. But the fact was, your dad *was* there, and even if I had wanted to throw away our friendship to get in the middle of them, it wouldn't have mattered. So I settled for being a friend, and that worked for a long time."

"Until when?" Meghan spit out the words. "Until Daddy was sick? Or before that?"

"Meghan. Stop and think about what you're saying. I know you're emotional right now, but try to be reasonable. Did you ever see anything between your mom and me, all these years? Anything but friendship? No. And not even in the year since your dad died. But I'll be straight with you. Watching your mom cope with everything after Daniel died, seeing how strong she was, how she was there for everyone, including you and Joseph and all of the posse, that made me fall in love with her all over again."

Meghan heaved a sigh but didn't speak.

"Still, I might never have made a move, but then the posse started talking about one of us taking care of Jude. I guess maybe I felt like I had approval to do something I had wanted to do for a long time. I moved kind of slow, because I wasn't sure how your mom felt. But then. . ." I paused. What had happened with Jude that night in the bar was not something I was willing to share with her daughter. Some things were better kept private.

"But then it turned out, to my amazement, that your mom could feel the same way about me. We weren't trying to hide it from you and Joseph. We just wanted to tell you in person. This is new, and it probably feels to you like it's moving fast."

"You think?" Meghan's bitterness came through both tone and words. "Couldn't you just keep being friends?"

"Spoken like someone who's never really been in love." I smiled. "We *are* still friends, Meggie. We always will be. But we're also in love. I'm sure you don't want to think about that, because kids rarely want to know that their parents still have those kinds of feelings. But it's the truth."

She turned her head away, mouth tight.

"I have two things you need to hear, Meghan, and then I'll leave you be to think things over. The first is this. Your dad taught me a lot over the years, but the last lesson was the most important. It's that we never know how much time we have, so we can't go around thinking that there will always be a tomorrow to do what we want or what we know we should. Your mother and I aren't teenagers, though you're probably thinking we're acting like we are. I don't know how long we'll have together, but I am damn sure going to take advantage of every moment.

"And here's the second. You have a family who loves you, and who you love. They're not perfect, and maybe they don't always live up to your standards. But they're yours, better or worse. Lindsay is the mother of your nephew. Whether she and Joseph get married or not, whether things work out and they stay together or not, she's part of your family now. Start treating her like it. I know you, Meggie. You can be the sweetest girl, the one anyone would want in his corner. Be in Joseph's corner. Be in your mom's corner. Don't be someone who stands in the way of their happiness."

I shoved back my chair, rinsed out his mug and swung out the kitchen door.

Chapter Twenty-Five

Jude

IT HAD BEEN A HELL of a morning, and it was only ten o'clock. I scraped off the grill, scowling at it. My eyes were red and puffy, and my whole body ached from the sleep I'd missed, tossing and turning last night.

The breakfast crowd had been particularly demanding, and Sadie was snapping at everyone. I sniffled and ran an arm over my forehead. I was sweaty and grimy and wanted to go home.

Only I knew going home wouldn't really help, because Meghan was there, sulking and huffing around the house. I briefly considered running away, fantasizing about a beach that was far away from my own sand and surf.

"Look at my gorgeous woman."

Wrapped up in my own misery, I hadn't heard Logan come in. I looked over my shoulder and rolled her eyes.

"You need glasses. I'm a mess."

"Maybe, but you're my beautiful mess. Do you have a minute?"

I blew at a piece of hair that had drooped over my eyes. "Not really. Still getting through the end of the breakfast run and lunch is at my heels."

"Okay, then, we'll do this here." Ignoring the grease and flakes of charred food dotting my skin, Logan took my hands in his own and drew me close.

"Logan, you're going to get all nasty!"

He smiled. "Maybe later, baby. For now, shut up and listen."

I snapped my lips closed, green eyes wide and wondering as I stared at him.

"Judetha Rivers Hawthorne, I love you. I have always loved you, and I will always love, from now until the end of forever. Will you please, please, do me the honor of becoming my wife?"

The griddle scraper fell to the floor with a clatter. I stood, still as a statue, my eyes never leaving Logan's face.

"I know this is fast, and I know you're not sure if you want to be married again. But I'm asking you, Jude. Do this for me. I want to be married, and I want to be married to you. And I don't want to think about it for months. I want to live every moment we have together, for as long as that might be."

My breath was somehow caught in my throat. The noise of the restaurant faded so that all I could hear was Logan. All I could see were his shining eyes, brimming with love.

Every reason I might have had for not saying yes, or even for saying an outright no, fled from my mind. There was only Logan, with his steadfast heart and his constancy, and only one word I heard coming from my mouth.

"Yes."

Surprise dawned on Logan's face, swiftly replaced by pure

joy. He took my face in his hands and lowered his mouth to mine.

Every bit of love, anticipation and desire that he'd ever felt for me was poured into one kiss. It began softly and sweetly, and then moved to possession and heat as he coaxed my lips open, lazing his tongue within my mouth to stroke and tease.

When he finally released my lips, Logan grabbed me around the waist and lifted me in his arms. He gave a yell that reverberated through the Rip Tide and out the open windows onto the beach as he spun me.

All conversation in the restaurant ceased, and Sadie stopped in mid-step. Every eye swiveled to the kitchen and the crazy couple locked in an embrace in front of the half-cleaned griddle.

"What in the hell do you crazy people think you're doing?" Sadie stomped around the bar, fire in her eyes.

Logan held tight to me, as I giggled and buried my face in his shoulder. "Sadie, she said yes! This beautiful, sexy, amazing woman just agreed to marry me. I think a little shouting is order, don't you?"

Sadie's face broke into a broad grin. "Well, if that's all. Carry on." She swung back to the gawking customers. "What are y'all looking at? Get back to your eating."

"Champagne on the house!" Logan called. "Mimosas all around." A cheer rolled over the room.

"Are you nuts? You're going to make me go broke." I shook my head but couldn't hide my smile.

"Yes, I'm nuts, and don't worry, I'll cover the champagne.

I think the owner will give me break on the cost." He leaned to whisper in my ear. "She's crazy about me."

"She definitely is." I held my hand to his cheek and kissed him senseless. "But I'm not sure she'll ever forgive you for proposing when she's covered in grease and sweat."

Logan brushed my hair back and smiled down me her. "I didn't want to waste another minute of my life without you. All of you. Grease, sweat, kids, grandkid. . .I want it all."

It took two hours for everything in the bar to calm down, and by then, the lunch rush had begun. The crowd swelled as word of our engagement spread; locals stopped in just to see if it were true and to offer their best. They jostled in line with the tourists.

I never stopped moving, and I never stopped smiling.

The hustle and bustle was just beginning to slow down when I turned to see my daughter walk into the restaurant. Part of me wanted to rush over and hug Meggie tight, but I held back, letting her come to her.

Meghan stopped just within the kitchen, beyond the bar. She was twisting the strap of her purse within her fingers.

"Mom? Do you have a minute?"

I set down the bread I had been about to toast. I turned to Logan, who had jumped in to help cook and serve.

"Can you finish this order?" I pointed to the slip of paper and then glanced at Meghan.

Logan's eyes flicked to follow my gaze. He moved to pick up the bread. "Sure. Hey, Meggie."

Uncertainty flashed on the girl's face. "Hey, Uncle Logan."

She licked her lips. "Um, I didn't thank you for the coffee this morning."

Logan shrugged. "No problem. Your mom made it, I just poured it." He winked at her, and I could feel an easing of the tension around us.

I led my daughter out onto the deck, to a corner table removed from the customers. Sinking into a chair, I sighed and propped my feet on another seat.

"It's been a long morning." I looked out over the beach. "Such a pretty day, lots of people in town."

"Yeah." Meggie bit her lip and took a deep breath. "Mom, I'm sorry. About yesterday. I acted like a brat."

I closed my eyes, relief overpowering me. "Yeah, you kind of did, honey. But you know what? We all do that, at one time or another. The important part is how you make it up."

Meghan nodded. "I know. Uncle Logan talked to me this morning. I didn't want to listen, I didn't want him to be right, but I did, and he was. So I talked to Joseph for a long time. And I apologized to Lindsay, too. I even offered to babysit tonight, so they can go out by themselves." She shrugged. "I figured it was the least I could do."

I rose and knelt by my little girl, pulling her into a tight hug. "I'm proud of you, Meggie. And thank you." I drew back, looked up into the eyes that were so like my own.

"Meggie, about Uncle Logan. I want you to hear it from me. He proposed this morning. And I said yes."

To my shock, Meghan began to laugh.

"That's funny?"

She shook her head. "It's just that I was so rude, Mom. I

was really a bitch. And let's face it, our family is kind of screwed up right now. If Uncle Logan chose this minute to ask you to marry him, he must really love you."

I grinned. "You've got a point."

∝⊙

Dinner that night was an entirely different occasion. Logan had snagged a bottle of champagne from the Tide. Joseph grilled chicken, and Lindsay and Meghan chased me out of the kitchen while they cooked.

"Here." Lindsay plunked the baby on my lap. "You two stay out of trouble. Let us take care of you for once."

We ate around the patio table, passing the baby from lap to lap to give Lindsay and Joseph a break. As the meal wound down, Joseph stood, lifting his glass.

"I want to make a toast." He cleared his throat, and looking around the table, blinking back tears.

"To my mom and dad, who made this family, crazy as it is. Dad, we know you're always with us. Mom, you've kept us together and been strong for so long. We all love you." He shifted his eyes to Logan as I felt tears trickle down my cheeks.

"And to Uncle Logan, who is insane enough to take us on. Thanks for seeing beyond the crazy. We love you, too." Joseph raised his glass and drank.

"Here, here." The rest of us followed suit, and even baby DJ gurgled in agreement.

Chapter Twenty-Six

Jude

"I HAVE A QUESTION."

I raised my head to look at Logan. We were lying in his bed, drowsing in the aftermath of what he had called proposal sex.

After dinner was cleaned up, Meggie had insisted that everyone needed to go out. She was babysitting, and she wanted DJ all to herself. Joseph and Lindsay decided to see a movie in Elson. Logan and I didn't tell anyone where we planned to go or what we planned to do.

"I already answered your question." My lips curved into a smile. "I said yes. Actually, I think I said it quite a few times tonight."

"Smartass." He chucked me under the chin. "No, this is another question. Or maybe more like an idea."

"I'm listening." I snuggled into his side as his arm tightened around me. He picked up my hand as it lay on his chest and toyed with my fingers.

"You're still wearing Daniel's ring."

"Yes." I was silent for a moment as we both looked at the band of gold. "I thought about that today. I was glad you didn't have an engagement ring for me yet, because I hadn't taken this one off. It would have been awkward."

"But it doesn't have to be." Logan rolled a little so he could see my face clearly. He propped his head in his hand, elbow on the bed.

"Here's my idea. Why don't you give Joseph your engagement ring from Daniel, let him give that to Lindsay? It'll mean a lot to both of them. But keep your wedding ring."

I raised my eyebrows. "Keep it?"

"Yes, keep wearing it. And when we get married—which is going to be soon—I'll give you my wedding ring, and you can add it on your finger. The way I look at it is Daniel will always be with us. He's part of us. Why try to pretend he isn't? Let's acknowledge it."

Tears brimmed in my eyes, and I wriggled closer to Logan, lifting my lips to his.

"That is the most beautiful thing I've ever heard. You may have just won yourself another round of proposal sex."

"Really?" Logan's eyes gleamed. "Well, hold on then, because I've got something else." He rolled away from me, opened his nightstand drawer and drew out a black velvet box. Without saying a word, he placed it in my hand.

"What's this?" I looked up at him in confusion. "I thought you didn't have a ring yet."

"No," Logan corrected. "I said I didn't have the ring *with* me this morning. I bought this the morning after the limoncello."

TAWDRA KANDLE

I rolled my eyes. "Is that what we're always going to call the first night we made love? The limoncello night?"

"Works for me. I owe that yellow stuff a lot. Remind me to send your uncle John a big thank you note." He motioned to the box. "Are you going to open it?"

I flipped the lid up and drew in a deep breath. "Oh, Logan. It's gorgeous."

The ring was an emerald, a gleaming perfect round green stone set in the midst of clustered diamonds on a platinum band.

"I figured you'd already had a diamond once, and emeralds always make me think of your eyes." He smiled and took the ring from the box. "May I?"

I nodded wordlessly. With great care, Logan eased off the simple diamond solitaire that had been on my finger for over twenty years and placed it in the now-empty ring box. He slid the emerald ring into its place.

We lay together, admiring it on me. Logan held my hand to his mouth and kissed each finger.

"For the rest of ever," he whispered before he rolled over to cover my body again.

⌐⊙

Meghan headed back to school early on Monday morning, after extracting a promise from her brother that he, Lindsay and DJ would visit Savannah soon.

"And you're coming back for the weddings, right?" Lindsay asked. "I know Clearwater is a long drive, but my parents really want us to get married down there." Joseph had wasted no time; my diamond solitaire now glistened on Lindsay's hand.

"Two fall beach weddings!" Meggie rolled her eyes. "Don't you people know how many exams I have coming up? You're going to wreck havoc on my GPA." But she smiled as she said it.

Later that morning, as Sadie and I finished up with the breakfast crowd, Joseph ambled in the door.

"Where's that baby?" Sadie demanded, looking over his shoulder.

"I remember when *I* was the one you wanted to see." Joseph sighed. "Sorry, Sadie. Lindsay took him over to visit Aunt Samantha." He glanced at me. "You have a minute to talk?"

"Sure." I untied my apron. "Out on the deck?"

"Nah, right here at the bar is good. I'd like Sadie here, too."

Sadie climbed onto a stool. "I never say no to sit-down. What's on your mind?"

Joseph licked his lips and took a deep breath. "I've been thinking about this for a while. Mom, I know I need to finish school, and I'm going to. But not in Gainesville. Lindsay and I are going to enroll here, at the community college."

I smiled. "That's great, honey. I'm glad to hear it."

"But here's the thing. We're going to need some place to live, and jobs so we can support ourselves and the baby. When I was at lunch with Uncle Logan, he mentioned he hoped you could get someone to cover mornings for you here at the Tide someday, to free you up a little. So I got to thinking. What if I took over mornings at the Tide for you? Most mornings, at least. I could do that and still get to take classes. And between

Lindsay and me, we could maybe take over a few other shifts, wherever you needed us."

I didn't answer at once. "Are you sure you want to do that? Four o'clock comes early, especially when you have a baby at home."

"You did it, Mom." Joseph grinned. "And here's part two. If I were working here, maybe Lindsay, DJ and I could live upstairs. Maybe that could be part of my salary, you know. Free rent. And then it wouldn't be so hard to get up and do the opening."

I nodded. "You've given this a lot of thought. What does Lindsay say?"

"She thinks it's a great idea. She loves the Tide, and she really wants to settle in the Cove. Uncle Logan even mentioned that maybe she could help out at the new bed and breakfast, once it's open."

I looked at Sadie. The older woman gazed at Joseph, and in her eyes, I could see the dawning acceptance that this boy, whom we had both watched grow since he was an infant, was now a man.

Finally, Sadie turned back to me. "Seems like a no-brainer to me. Gives the boy what he needs for his new family, frees you up to have a little of a life now with your new man." She spread her hands, wrinkled and gnarled, on the bar. "And Mack and I will be here to make sure none of you screw this place up."

Joseph smiled and looked at me. "Well? What do you think?"

I rose and hugged my son. "I think you've got yourself a deal."

Chapter Twenty-Seven

Jude

HAWTHORNE HOUSE OPENED TEN DAYS later, right on schedule. The whole town turned out for the celebration.

Joseph and Lindsay covered The Rip Tide that day so that I could play hostess at the bed and breakfast. I stood with Logan on the front porch, greeting friends, visitors and guests, smiling until I thought my face would crack.

"Do you know what it means to me to have you here right now?" Logan murmured into my ear. "It's more than I ever could have dreamed when I was designing this place, putting it back together."

I leaned my head on his shoulder. "I guess Hawthorne House is kind of like us. Old stuff put together in new ways."

"Hey, speak for yourself. I'm not old, and I'm willing to prove it." He winked at me. "There's got to be one bed upstairs that's not being used."

"I doubt it. We're full to capacity, and I've heard only good comments so far. Of course, that's probably because Abby and Emmy are working their asses off."

I glanced through the door, where she could see Abby chatting with guests in the sitting room, while Emmy passed another tray of cookies in the dining room. Cooper stood near the wall, talking to an older woman about his furniture designs, but I noticed his eyes followed Emmy as she wove among chairs and people.

"So far, so good." Logan linked our fingers and kissed the back of my hand. "The portrait of Daniel should be ready by next month. But the photo Joseph picked out looks good for now."

"It does." I closed her eyes and sighed. "My feet are killing me. How much longer do you think we need to be here? Seems like things are slowing a little now."

"Come on. I have an idea." Logan tugged my hand and led me down the porch steps and around the side of the house, past the fragrant jasmine that crept up the side of the chimney, into the backyard. A few people wandered there, admiring the fountain or the neat beds of flowers, but for the most part, it was empty.

We crossed to a bench that sat secluded among the trees, and I sat down with grateful exhale.

"Better?" Logan pulled my feet onto his lap, removed my shoes and began rubbing my feet.

"Much. Ahhh. Keep that up, we might have to kick guests out of one of those beds, after all."

Logan quirked an eyebrow at me. "Sounds like a plan." He

massaged up my legs, tantalizing as he reached further onto my thigh.

I leaned my head back and hummed in appreciation.

"Speaking of rooms, I have a surprise for you. One I hope you'll like."

"Really?" Smiling sleepily, I captured one of his hands, holding it in my own.

"I told Abby to put aside a room for us for two nights in October. For our wedding night, and to kick off our honeymoon."

"Oh, Logan, really? That's perfect." I swung my legs down and scooted closer to him. "Thank you. I couldn't imagine any better place to spend our first night together. Married, I mean."

"And then, a week in New Orleans. You'll love the city. Think of it, a week with nothing to do. . .but me." He waggled his eyebrows at me suggestively, and Jude laughed.

"I can't promise I won't call Joseph every day to check on the Tide, but I will try to be carefree. How's that?"

"As long as it's you and me, together, I don't even care." He brought his mouth down to mine again, this time deepening our kiss, coaxing me even closer.

"I have a surprise for you, too." I spoke against his lips.

"Right here and now?" Logan's eyes gleamed, and I pushed against his chest.

"No, that comes later. This is different. But since we're talking about plans and the future. . ." I shifted to see him better. "I listed my house with a rental agent."

Logan blinked. "You did? When?"

"This week. She already has some interested renters. I know we talked about selling it, but if I don't have to, I'd rather not."

"Are you trying to keep your options open?"

I rolled my eyes. "Not at all. I was thinking, though, that at some point, if Joseph and Lindsay stay in the Cove, that apartment might become too small for them. They might want a bigger place. And since you and Daniel designed and built that house for me, I'd like it to stay in the family. Does that make sense?"

"Absolutely." He drew me in, kissing my forehead. "So that just leaves one more question."

I tilted my head. "Which is?"

"When are you moving in with me?"

I smiled, my eyes inviting. "I was thinking tonight."

Epilogue

THEY GATHERED ON A PERFECT afternoon in late October. The sun was still strong, but a cooling breeze from the ocean made the air just right. Above the gleaming white sand, the sky was deep blue, without even one cloud to mar its beauty.

The old dance pavilion had been decorated with draped cloth in green and yellow. Bunches of sunflowers filled vases at one end, and there were seashells scattered on the tables that surrounded the narrow aisle.

All the chairs that circled those tables were filled. On each table sat a tall clear bottle of limoncello.

The posse sat front and center, beaming in happy expectation. Janet wiped at her eyes as Eric held her other hand. Samantha grinned smugly as Sandra and Matt exchanged secretive smiles. Cooper sighed as he watched his daughter gaze around with starry eyes.

At the table behind them, Emmy kept her children quiet as she chatted with Abby.

Violin music played as first Meghan and then Lindsay walked down the aisle. They wore green, in different shades and styles, and Lindsay carried Daniel Joseph, dressed in an adorable little tuxedo. He looked around with wide eyes at all the people who ohh'd when they saw him.

Logan stepped to the front, wearing a simple gray suit. Mark stood up with him as his best man, representing the entire posse.

At his nod, the violin music ceased, and the opening strains of *Crazy For You* began to play. Sadie, in her role as mother of the bride, rose to her feet, yanking Mack up to join her. Everyone else followed.

Jude stepped over the dunes, holding onto Joseph's arm. She wore a simple long dress in a deep green that nearly matched her eyes and complimented the dark hair that fell in waves around her shoulders.

Her eyes never left Logan's as she walked toward him. Years of friendship and love seemed to converge in this place where both past and future met and meshed.

When they reached the front of the pavilion, Joseph kissed her cheek before he stepped back to join Lindsay and the baby.

Logan took her hand, lacing his fingers with hers. As they turned to face the minister who would join them in the eyes of God, an oddly soft breeze swept around them, offering a blessing and a benediction of its own.

Jude smiled up at Logan, and they began their forever.

The Posse Play List

Jude loves music, especially tunes from her teenage
years—which would be the 1980's. It was a pleasure to
enjoy some of these songs again while writing her story.
Lots of memories there!
And Jimmie, I still always look for you when Crazy For You
begins to play.

1985 . . .Bowling For Soup
If She Knew What She Wants. . .The Bangles
Let's Go Crazy. . .Prince
Our Lips Are Sealed. . .The Go-Go's
We Belong. . .Pat Benatar
The Glamorous Life. . .Sheila E.
The Tide is High. . .Blondie
Dancing in the Dark. . .Bruce Springsteen
Come On, Eileen. . .Dexy's Midinght Runner
White Wedding. . .Billy Idol
Modern Love. . .David Bowie
Only the Good Die Young. . .Billy Joel
Rock the Casbah. . .The Clash
Crazy For You. . .Madonna

Acknowledgements

2020

Crystal Cove is a fictional town, but it's always going to be one of my favorite places in the world.

The Posse was my first contemporary romance. It was my first adult book. It was my first non-paranormal novel. I wrote it very quickly in 2013, and by the end, I had fallen in love with all of the characters. I knew who was going to have their own books down the road.

I wrote five other books set in or connected to Crystal Cove: *The Plan, The Path, Underneath My Christmas Tree, Love Me Home* and *The Problem.* And I also wrote a connected series Love in a Small Town—the first book in that series is Meghan's story.

Seven years after its release, though, it bothered me that for some reason, I wrote The Posse in the third person. It is my only book not in the first person. As I prepared to package it for the Crystal Cove Romances Volume 1, I decided to fix that.

That's why the book you just read is in the first person. I made a few other small tweaks as I re-worked it. But what pleased me the most was that the story held up. Jude and Logan and the rest of the posse . . . they still make me smile, bring tears to my eyes and make me sigh.

Crystal Cove is based on New Smyrna Beach, Florida, but of course, that place is only my jumping off point. All characters are fictional. Still, when I visit New Smyrna, I sometimes think I might see Jude behind the bar at the restaurant on which the Tide is based. I swear I catch glimpses of Emmy and Abby outside the B&B . . . and I might even have heard Logan's voice as I walked down the beach.

I hope that you'll enjoy the other Crystal Cove Romances—including those yet to come!

With much love always. <3

The Original Acknowledgements (2013)

Stepping into a new genre is a scary proposition. One day, as I worked on finishing *Endless*, the final book of The King Series, I was driving home from the beach, and *The Posse* fell into my lap, fully formed. This is very unusual for me; generally, I meet a character and slowly discover her history, her story. But with Jude, I felt compelled to write her book, and I knew the details from beginning to end.

Since I have a fairly full publishing schedule, choosing to drop a new book into the lineup wasn't easy. I did it anyway, and I am so glad I did.

I could not do what I do without the support and encouragement of my business partner and friend, Mandie Stevens. She tells me hard truths and keeps me on the straight and narrow, and she has taught me more about the business of being an author than I could ever imagine. Plus she lets me whine, gripe and vent whenever the need arises. I love you, my friend!

And the rest of my PBT family—particularly Amanda Long, Jen Rattie and Stacey Blake—you are fabulous. I love you all. We have the best team in the world, and I can't imagine doing any of this without you.

Our bloggers are amazing. They are professional, encouraging and some of the best people I've ever met. Thank you for your support.

I mentioned Stacey Blake above, but I have to give her even more kudos. She has jumped into proof-reading, editing and formatting in addition to all the work she does for us at PBT. I truly believe there is nothing she cannot do. She also has taken on many of my admin tasks, freeing me to write. This book would not exist if not for her hard work.

The fearless and feckless ladies of Romantic Edge Books are the most sharing, wonderful, words-cannot-describe-them group of writers in existence. Ready to take on the world?

Up until the publication of my first book, I was always Mommy first. Consequently, my family has had to learn a new normal, as I am not always around, and even when I'm physically here, I might not be mentally present. They have handled it with grace and humor, and I love them for it, as well as for their constant cheerleading and support.

My husband inspires me each and every day. He has always been the first one to believe that I can do anything. Sometimes that's a little frightening, but most days, it's just the push I need.

To my readers . . .your messages, your love for my characters and stories, have been life changing. Thanks for going with me into this new world. I promise we haven't abandoned King.

About the Author

Photo: Heather Batchelder

Tawdra Kandle writes romance, in just about all its forms. She loves unlikely pairings, strong women, sexy guys, hot love scenes and just enough conflict to make it interesting. Her books include new adult and adult contemporary romance; under the pen name Tamara Kendall, she writes paranormal romance, and under the pen name Tessa Kent, she writes erotic romance. Tawdra lives in central Florida with her husband, two sweet pups and too many cats. Assorted grown children and a perfect granddaughter live nearby. And yeah, she rocks purple hair.

Subscribe to Tawdra's newsletter to keep up with all of her releases and sales!
tawdrakandle.com/websitenlsub

And check out her non-Facebook reader group,
The Inside Squad.
tawdras-inside-squad.mn.co/landing?space_id=2170332

Facebook
www.facebook.com/AuthorTawdraKandle

Twitter
twitter.com/tawdra

Website
tawdrakandle.com

Other Books

For more information on Tawdra's books and buy links to all vendors, please visit Tawdra's website at tawdrakandle.com.

Diagnosis: Love Medical Romances
Pretend You're Mine
Informed Consent
Internal Fixation
Intensive Care
Implicit Memory
Til We Part
Intentional Grounding
Ineligible Receiver
Illegal Touching

The Anti-Cinderella Chronicles
The Anti-Cinderella
The Anti-Cinderella Takes London
The Anti-Cinderella Conquers the World
The Anti-Cinderella Royal Romance Box Set

The Anti-Cinderella World Romances

Fifty Frogs

Hot Off The Press

The Cuffing Season

A Dozen Dreams (Coming Soon!)

Sort of Sleeping Beauty (Coming Soon!)

Slightly Snow White (Coming Soon!)

Love in a Small Town

Love Me Home (A LIAST Prequel)

The Last One

The First One

The Only One

The Perfect One

The Wild One

The Always One

The Hard One

My One and Always

The Forever One

The Love Song One

The Meant To Be One

Love in a Small Town Volume I

Love in a Small Town Volume II

A Year of Love in a Small Town
A New Year in a Small Town
Be My Valentine in a Small Town
My Lucky Day in a Small Town
Hoppy Easter in a Small Town
May You Be Mine in a Small Town
My Big Fat Prom Date in a Small Town
Make Me See Fireworks in a Small Town
Fall in Love in a Small Town
Be My Boo in a Small Town
Thankful for You in a Small Town
Merry and Bright in a Small Town

Crystal Cove Romances
The Posse
The Plan
The Path
Underneath My Christmas Tree
The Problem
The Crystal Cove Romance Box Set

The Keeping Score Trilogy
Young (A Keeping Score Prequel)
False Start
Three & Out
The Comeback Route
The Keeping Score Box Set

Making the Score Series
Down By Contact
Next Man Up
Game of Inches

The Career Soldier Series
Maximum Force
Temporary Duty
Hitting the Silk
Zone of Action
Damage Assessment
Scheme of Maneuver
Evergreen
Army Blue
The Career Soldier Collection
The Mustang (West Point Tour of Duty)
The Rotorhead (West Point Tour of Duty)
The Shavetail (West Point Tour of Duty)

The Perfect Dish Romances
Best Served Cold
Just Desserts
I Choose You
Just Roll With It

Books Written As Tessa Kent

Good Vibrations
More Than Words
Baby, I'm Yours
Save It For Me

Small Town Swingers
Welcome to Paradise
Night Moves
The Heat Is On
Fading Into You

Third Date Rule Romances
Crush
Crave
Crescendo
Tease
Tempt
Take

Tiny Bit Taboo
The Conference Taboo
The Ex In-Law Taboo
The Business Trip Taboo
The Client Taboo

Books Written as Tamara Kendall

The King Quartet (Young Adult)
Fearless
Breathless
Restless
Endless
The King Series Box Set

Serendipity
Undeniable
Stardust on the Sea
Unquenchable
The Shadow Bells
Moonlight on the Meadow
The Fox's Wager

Recipe for Death
Death Fricassee
Unforgettable
Death A La Mode
Death Over Easy
The Recipe for Death Box Set
Age Of Aquarius
The Save Tomorrow Collection

Printed in Great Britain
by Amazon